"Thank you for rescuing me, Tom."

Bec spoke softly, the sound evaporating so quickly it was almost as if the words had not been said. But the echo of the message resonated loud and clear, vibrating in his chest.

Tilting her head forward, she pressed her lips gently against his cheek.

The touch was brief, a light caress. But the softness and warmth of her lips sent a riot of sensation ricocheting through him, making every part of him vibrate with suppressed longing.

She trusts me. The warning sounded faintly in the recesses of his mind.

She wants me.

Six weeks of concealed emotions exploded inside him, pushing every rational thought from his head. He couldn't hold back any longer. He needed her arms around his neck, her legs around his waist, her lips against his own. He needed her now like he needed air.

Dear Reader,

Have you ever watched a movie and come away from it saying, "I am *going* to visit that place"? I have. The memory of the jade waters of Halong Bay in the film *Indochine* stayed with me long after the credits had faded. A couple of years later, when a friend came home raving about Vietnam, I booked a holiday.

Vietnam sends you into sensory overload. The sound of horns, the smell of fish sauce and lemongrass, the chaos of people continuously on the move, the spectacular scenery and the friendliness of the people—all of it sucks you into its welcoming vortex.

This got me thinking about a romance set in this beautiful country. Bec, an Australian nurse, comes to Vietnam determined to help the children of the country and escape the memory of her own troubled childhood. She has decided that it's safest not to love, and is creating an independent life for herself. But she meets Tom, a dedicated doctor. He is Eurasian. Born in Vietnam, raised in Australia and feeling as if he does not belong in either country, he is working in Vietnam and trying to trace his birth mother. He feels his life is on hold until he knows more about himself. Together they challenge each other's beliefs about themselves as they travel around Vietnam dealing with medical emergencies.

Just as Halong Bay wove its magic over me, it weaves a special magic over Tom and Bec. But is magic enough to keep them together? I hope you enjoy traveling through Vietnam, and perhaps you might book yourself a holiday there as well. Let me know!

Love,

Fiona x

A WOMAN TO BELONG TO
Fiona Lowe

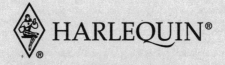

TORONTO • NEW YORK • LONDON
AMSTERDAM • PARIS • SYDNEY • HAMBURG
STOCKHOLM • ATHENS • TOKYO • MILAN • MADRID
PRAGUE • WARSAW • BUDAPEST • AUCKLAND

ISBN-13: 978-0-373-06633-9
ISBN-10:   0-373-06633-3

A WOMAN TO BELONG TO

First North American Publication 2007

This edition published by arrangement with Harlequin Books S.A.

® and TM are trademarks of the publisher. Trademarks indicated with
® are registered in the United States Patent and Trademark Office, the
Canadian Trade Marks Office and in other countries.

www.eHarlequin.com

Printed in U.S.A.

A WOMAN TO BELONG TO

To Caroline, Deb, Gayle, Karen and Mon.
Thanks for the laughs, the company
and the great tennis.

And to Gayle for her wonderful travel tales and
inspiring our visit to Vietnam.

CHAPTER ONE

RAIN TUMBLED FROM the sky, a wall of pure water—the response of humidity finally reaching breaking point. Bec Monahan tilted her head back, enjoying the refreshing coolness on her face. A moment later she sighed.

Hanoi traffic, chaotic under perfect conditions, would now be at gridlock. No point getting a taxi. She glanced around. No cyclos either—all the drivers had retreated to shelter. *Damn.*

Pulling her *non la* forward she smiled at the varied uses of the traditional Vietnamese conical hat. Just an hour ago she'd been using it as a fan and a much-needed sunshade. Now it doubled as an umbrella. It also screamed tourist or country hick in the emerging cosmopolitan city.

She didn't care. Two days after arriving and immediately sweating in tight Western clothing, she'd adopted the local dress of light cotton trousers and a long-sleeved blouse. The outfit was practical, comfortable and plain. She stood out enough just by being Australian, and this way she drew less attention. She'd learned from an early age it was safer to fade into the background.

She peered at the scrawled address as the rain blurred the blue ink, making it run across the page. She bit her lip and sent up a hopeful plea that this time the address was correct. Tracking down Dr Thông had turned into a marathon.

Weaving her way around the impromptu food stalls and parked motorcycles, she turned into a street clearly marked by an enamelled street sign, a legacy from the French occupation. She stopped abruptly. A shiver raced across her skin as a wave of goose-bumps rose in warning.

A dead-end narrow lane. *Always have an escape route.*

Life with her father had taught her that. Never let yourself be cornered. She breathed in deeply. This was a leafy suburb of Hanoi. *But you know what leafy suburbs can hide.*

'Madame?'

Bec started and turned.

A young man with an umbrella came toward her, concern crossing his face.

'*Bác sǐ.* Doctor.' Bec repeated the oft-said phrase wondering how bad her accent sounded to the locals.

The young man grinned a trade-mark wide Vietnamese smile and pointed to the gate in the high wall at the end of the lane. 'He is there.'

Bec smiled, nodding her head in thanks, and ran the last few metres to the gate. Her heart hammered against her ribs in anticipation. Finally, after two days of searching, she was making progress. Since arriving in Vietnam on holiday, she'd had an increasing sense of needing to contribute to this glorious country. To do *something* for the children of Vietnam. At night she lay in bed and tried to work out the best way to help. One week ago she'd decided that a clinic which combined health and education was the best way to go.

Healthy children had a greater capacity to learn and children who had access to education had a greater chance to improve their lives. Education opened up options even if it was just the option to flee an unsafe situation.

She'd used that option.

Now she wanted to give other kids the same chance. Australia had a lot of established services for children and Vietnam didn't. She hoped to use the ties Australia had with this nation to her advantage.

But trying to work out how to start the process of working with the Vietnamese health department and education department had almost defeated her. Each bureaucrat fobbed her off with, 'Talk to Dr Thông.' She had no idea who this doctor was but she was pinning her hopes on him. He must hold the key to her plan.

The heavy gate closed behind her. Suddenly she was in a tranquil courtyard; the noise and hustle of Hanoi receded to barely a buzz. Only the sound of heavy rain on the ground broke the peaceful serenity of this haven.

A French villa stood before her, its green shutters closed against the rain. Bec swore she could hear whispered stories of a life of decadent elegance before years of turmoil. She shook her head against a feeling of light-headedness. The heat and humidity must be getting to her.

Soaked to the skin, she tugged on the old door pull and a bell sounded in the distance.

She waited. The bell rang out. Silence descended.

Her stomach growled—hunger gnawing at nothing as anticipatory acid burned her stomach. She'd given away her breakfast of rice soup to a homeless child. She'd planned to grab something else but had got side-tracked with her search.

The world tilted slightly and she realised it was now mid-afternoon. *Stupid.* She needed to be on top of things when she met Dr Thông.

She pulled the bell again, her hand gripping the pulley tightly for support.

The bell chimed loud and long. Footsteps sounded.

Bec bowed her head and breathed in a calming breath. *This is it.*

The door creaked open and stilted Vietnamese swirled around her, the accent clumsy and unfamiliar.

She looked up quickly, her practised greeting dying on her lips.

She'd been expecting a short Vietnamese doctor. Instead, a tall, broad-shouldered man with designer tousled black hair filled the doorway, a backpack slung casually over one shoulder. He wore a well-known surfing-brand T-shirt, the spun cotton clinging like a second skin to a toned chest and muscular arms. A shadow of dark stubble highlighted a strong jaw and a firm mouth.

An unexpected quiver spread through her, racing down to her toes. She shook her head. She *really* needed some food. Blinking, she took another look at him through the rain. A sigh of dismay escaped her lips as her heart sank. This golden-skinned man belonged on a beach. He had tourist written all over him. He couldn't possibly be Dr Thông.

Large oval eyes, the colour of dark chocolate, studied her intently. 'Can I help you?'

The Australian accent stunned her and she searched for her voice. 'I'm sorry, I think I've been directed to the wrong place. I'm looking for Dr Thông.'

An ironic smile passed over high cheekbones. 'That's me. I'm Tom. It's written Thông, but pronounced Tom. Tom Bracken.' He hitched his backpack further up his shoulder. 'I'm also just leaving so you'd be better off trying the French hospital.'

Her brain stalled at his smile, driving away the confused thoughts of why he sounded and looked so Australian. She forced herself to focus. 'No, I'm not sick.'

'Glad to hear it. I'll be back in a few weeks so make an appointment with my housekeeper.'

Panic simmered in her belly. *Don't let him leave.* 'I need to talk to you about the orphans.'

He stiffened. 'Are you a journalist?'

She shook her head, confused, her mind racing to find a succinct sentence to make an impression on him and to stop him leaving right away. 'I'm a nurse.'

'Great. Again, try the French hospital.' He moved forward, towering over her meagre five feet and two inches.

She clenched her fists against the surge of unwanted fear that twisted inside her as she looked up at him. 'You don't understand. I'm not looking for a job.'

'So, you're not sick, you're not looking for a job and you're not a journalist.' His black eyebrows rose in perfect arches. 'Why do you need to see me?'

She swallowed hard, knowing what she said next

would either delay him or see him marching through the gate. 'I have a mission and I need your help.'

Don't stop, you'll miss your plane. Tom's grip on the doorhandle instinctively lessened as an irrational need to listen to this woman's story clashed with his desire to leave immediately.

Something in her voice made him pause. Energy and vitality rolled off her in waves, matched with a steely determination. Her chin jutted slightly as she stood her ground. He recognised that stance. He'd seen photos of himself doing the same thing.

When he'd opened the door and seen a petite woman in plain Vietnamese dress, with her head bowed against the rain, he'd immediately assumed she was a patient who'd been given the wrong address. Then she'd raised her face. The rush of heat that had whipped through him when her violet-blue eyes had caught his gaze still simmered inside him.

He'd never seen eyes that colour before. They reminded him of his mother's spring irises, the purple-blue flowers she insisted on growing despite the heat of the Australian bush.

And yet shadows lurked in the sparkle of vibrant colour. For a brief moment he had a crazy desire to chase those shadows away.

You don't have time for this, the pilot has a timetable. Ever since he'd been interviewed on local television, people had started approaching him, requesting his time for his perspective on health and his support for their own projects. And the local government officers referred to him anyone who asked about starting health programmes. He'd tried to convince them not to, but to no avail. He was flat out keeping up with his own patients and clinics, let alone taking on other people's work. His patients came first every time.

Thank goodness Jason, the PR person for Health For Life, was due back from his extended leave next week. He couldn't wait to hand over all the admin stuff and get back to focusing completely on medicine. His review of the rural outreach programme was overdue. He'd been jealously watching the other staff heading out around the country. Although he enjoyed the Hanoi hospital work, he'd missed his outreach work and the chance to assess new projects.

Water trickled down his neck, the droplets jerking him back to the present. For the first time since opening the front door he realised it was raining. *Remember the plane.* Dragging his gaze away from his visitor's mesmerising eyes, he countered the nagging voice inside his head. *Five minutes is all this will take.*

'Ms…?'

'Monahan. Rebecca Monahan, but please call me Bec.'

He smiled. 'You'd better come in out of the rain, Bec.'

'Thank you. I thought you'd never ask.' She took off her hat and long chestnut hair streaked with sun-kissed blonde cascaded down around her shoulders.

He stood stock-still, staring at her, completely captivated.

With a flick of her head, water bounced off her hair, spraying him. She giggled then smiled broadly, her face creasing in delicious laughter lines. 'Sorry, the monsoon and I are still adjusting to each other.'

She stepped forward, stopping abruptly when he didn't move, leaving a wide space between them. A flash of something lit her eyes and faded as fast as it had appeared.

He tried to catch it and read it, but it had vanished.

She tilted her head and raised her brows, her mouth pursing slightly. 'May I come in?'

Concentrate, Tom. 'Of course. Sorry.' He moved back, dropping his pack to the floor.

She walked into the entrance foyer, slightly favouring her left leg.

Tien, his housekeeper, used to people arriving at all times of the day and night, silently appeared holding a towel which she handed to Bec.

'Oh, dear, I'm dripping all over your floor.'

His country hospitality, drummed into him by his mother, came to the fore. 'Don't worry, that's why we have tiled floors. Would you like some lemon juice and water or tea? Something to eat?'

'Yes, please, I'm completely starving.' The moment she'd spoken she clapped her hands over her mouth like a child who believed she'd said the wrong thing. 'I'm sorry, I don't want to put you out.'

'Not at all. In Vietnam it's mandatory to over-feed all guests.' He grinned. 'Tien will be thrilled she has a willing recipient.' *Will you listen to yourself? Find out what she wants, and send her on her way.*

He ushered her into the sitting room. 'So, tell me about your mission.'

Her eyes sparkled like a child's, all innocence and wonder. 'I want to start a clinic and kindergarten for children.'

He suppressed a groan. He'd just given in to a crazy moment of attraction and let his guard down. *Fool.* Normally he was attuned to all the signs but somehow he'd let a naïve do-gooder into his house. He'd met plenty of people like this. They thought they could arrive from the West and change the world overnight. 'Why? Why do you want to start a clinic and a kinder?'

She started, disbelief creasing her brow. 'I thought that would be obvious.'

He folded his arms across his chest. 'How so?'

She threw her arms out in front of her in a dramatic gesture. 'There are kids here living in dire poverty, suffering from malnutrition and a host of childhood illnesses.'

His job was to play devil's advocate. He'd been burned before with bright ideas and no follow-through. 'Sure. Just like in many other parts of the world. So why here?'

She bit her lip and suddenly looked uncomfortable. 'You'll probably laugh.'

'Try me.'

She took in a deep breath, her breasts rising against her damp shirt.

A shock of unexpected lust rocked him and he forced his gaze to slide away. But an image of a curvaceous woman hidden under the baggy clothes had seared itself to his brain.

'I had a dream. Well, I had it more than once and now it's become a part of me—you know, a fire that won't be put out, an ache that won't be ignored.' Wide eyes implored him to understand.

Hell. He did. He knew that ache, that need that took hold and haunted you until you did something about it.

Even so, he didn't have time to get involved with a half-baked idea. He'd seen that happen over and over and his people didn't need to have their expectations raised, only to be dashed when the going got tough or homesickness hauled the do-gooder home.

'Why not make a donation to Health For Life? We're a nationwide agency and your money would be put to good use across the country. Then you've done your bit, helped out, eased your conscience.' He couldn't quite hide the condescension in his tone.

Her smiling mouth flattened into a firm line as her eyes flashed. 'My conscience isn't in question here. I have a vision for this project and I *will* be involved in a hands-on capacity.'

He grudgingly admired her determination but it was time to give her a reality check. 'And where did you think you would set up this clinic and kinder?'

'Here.'

'In Hanoi?'

She nodded. 'Yes.'

'Hanoi does have street kids, there's no disputing that. But what about the poverty-stricken areas in remote, rural Vietnam? The places where only one crop a year can be grown? Don't you think those children deserve your help?'

'Absolutely.'

'And how will you do that if you're working in Hanoi?'

She opened her mouth to speak but then closed it, wrinkling her nose in concentration.

Gotcha! He'd catch his plane to Lai Chau after all. 'Health For Life has the power behind it to work in many areas. Why reinvent the wheel? If you really want to help children then donating to us is probably the best way to go.'

You've got your projects to review and a plane to catch. Let Jason handle this. He rummaged through the bureau and found a business card. 'Here. Jason will be back next week and you can ring him then or contact the office in Australia when you get back from your holiday. Health For Life runs all sorts of programmes and you can choose one to donate to, or even work for one if you want to become involved.' He extended the card toward her.

She folded her arms across her chest, her eyes firing daggers in his direction. 'Why are you doing this?'

He ignored the edge of unease that hovered around his conscience and smiled. 'I'm happy to help where I can.'

Bec made a snorting sound. 'Help? You're fobbing me off big-time, Tom. It seems some people have the right to a vision while others of us don't.' She glared at him.

'Look, people come here on holiday and are confronted by what they see and they want to help. But life here wears most people down and they leave. Why start something you won't finish? I'm just trying to save you frustration and time.'

She started to pace. 'You're amazing. You know nothing about me and yet you've leapt to myriad conclusions. What gives you that right?'

Her words niggled, their grain of truth butting up against his self-righteous stance. 'I've seen too many people trying to save Vietnam. It doesn't need saving. It needs long-term commitment.'

She spun back to face him, staring him down. 'And you've made that commitment?'

He thought of his parents, both known and unknown. Of the pain and loss so many had endured. 'Yes, I have.'

'But you'll deny me that same opportunity.'

He shrugged, his discomfort about this conversation increasing by the minute. He was *not* going to tell a stranger his life story. 'My situation is completely different to yours.'

Her eyes flashed. 'How would you know? I don't know why you even asked me in from the rain. You should have just walked straight past me, rather than inviting me in with a closed mind.'

The barb hit, stinging in its accuracy. He'd let a pair of dancing eyes get under his guard and in the process had caused more disappointment than was necessary. Guilt seeped in.

She walked toward the door but stopped as Tien walked in with a steaming bowl of *pho*. The room immediately filled with the pungent aroma of coriander.

I'm completely starving. Her words slugged him. He couldn't let her leave on an empty stomach. 'Please, stay and eat your noodle soup.'

Emotions warred on her face and she almost seemed to slump, as if the fight had completely gone out of her.

A streak of self-righteousness curled inside him, tucked up neatly next to his guilt. He'd been on the money. Vietnam wasn't for the faint-hearted. If she couldn't survive an argument with him then she didn't have the gumption to face the challenges of working here.

She sat down with a smile of thanks for Tien, picked up the soup spoon and fork, and started to eat.

He watched her from the other side of the room, not wanting to but unable to stop himself. What the hell was wrong with him today? He met women all the time and didn't usually see past their job description to see the person. There was no point. His life was far too messy and complicated to be considering a relationship.

Inviting her in had been a bad idea. Well, he'd end it right. 'I'll call for a driver to take you back to your hotel as soon as you've finished your soup.'

'That would be the least you could do.' She shot him a derisive look. 'Tell me, Tom, you believe I have no idea about the real health needs of this country?'

He breathed deeply, not wanting to get into an argument. 'I don't think you have a full understanding of the big picture, no.'

She dextrously manoeuvred the noodles and pork into her mouth, her gaze fixed firmly on him, never wavering.

'And if I did my research, discovered the big picture, became familiar with the specific health needs of this country and developed a thorough plan of action…'

'Yes.' He nodded. 'That is exactly what you need to do.' Finally, she was realising what was really involved.

She nibbled on some coriander.

An image of her lips nibbling his flashed through his brain, completely unnerving him.

She had to go.

He had to catch a plane.

She smiled at him as she emptied the bowl. 'Sorry, I

won't hold you up any longer. You were on your way somewhere when I arrived?'

'I'm heading to the Lai Chau district.'

'The hill-tribe region, right?' A friendly tone had replaced the chill of a moment ago.

He gave an internal sigh of relief. She was seeing reason. 'That's right. I look after a clinic in a remote village there and I visit once a month. Local health workers staff it the rest of the time. I'll be doing some "train the trainer", as well as seeing patients. Right now we have a focus on maternal and child health.'

She reached for her hat and stood up. 'So is Lai Chau Province the sort of place I should visit to get a real feel for the country?'

'Sure. It would be a start.' He walked toward the door to usher her out.

'Excellent. My hotel is on the way to the airport and I can quickly grab my stuff.'

Her words ricocheted around his brain, trying to take purchase. 'Hang on a minute—you're not coming with me.'

She tilted her head slightly and focused her clear unflinching gaze straight at him. 'Why not? You said I needed to do my research and what better way than with a doctor who is completely familiar with the health needs?'

Indignation spluttered through him. 'I'm a doctor, not a tour guide!'

Her mouth took on the increasingly familiar firm line. 'And I'm a nurse, not a tourist. I'll pay my way and earn my keep. I have midwifery and maternal and child health qualifications, some emergency experience and a master's degree in public health. I'll be an asset, not a hindrance. Are you in the position of knocking back free professional help?'

Hell! She'd completely turned the tables on him. Somehow she'd seized control of the conversation without him realising.

He didn't want her travelling with him, with her sparkling eyes and wondrous smile. Part vixen, part ingénue, he hated the way his body reacted to her. He had to keep his focus firmly on his reasons for being in Vietnam. Between medicine and trying to trace his family, he had no time for anything else.

But how could he knock back an extra pair of medical hands? He didn't have the right when so many people had so little access to health care. A few weeks in the remote regions of the country would prove if she had the mettle to follow her dream.

He picked up his pack. 'It's hot and exhausting out there.'

A laugh quickly chased away her grimace. 'Tell me something I don't know.'

He had to regain some equilibrium, set some ground rules. 'You acknowledge I'm the doctor in charge?'

She nodded, her face serious, but a hint of a smile hovered about her mouth. 'Absolutely.'

So why didn't that ready agreement make him feel any more in control?

CHAPTER TWO

BEC LEANED AGAINST the supporting stilts of the thatched hut, which doubled as a clinic. She watched the scrawny bronze-coloured chickens pecking at the sun-baked earth, ever hopeful of finding some seed. Fanning herself with her hat, she was taking a five-minute breather from unpacking the medical supplies Tom had brought with them.

The bone-shaking four-wheel-drive journey to get to this small village, snuggled deep into the valley between towering rugged mountains, had taken five hours. The flight in the tiny plane to Lai Chau yesterday had been luxurious in comparison.

Her hand still ached from gripping the grab-handle above the window of the vehicle, trying to avoid being thrown against Tom or into his lap. Terror lanced her at the secret knowledge that it might not have been an awful experience if she *had* landed there.

But it would have been bad. Really bad. She couldn't trust her instincts when it came to men. She got it so wrong every time. First her father and then Nick. Both of them had only given pain, not love. She rubbed the ache in her leg. She carried the legacy of her time spent with both of them every day.

She avoided men as much as she could, both professionally and personally. *Keep a safe distance.* That had been her mode of operation since she was twenty. Anxiety-generated sweat broke out on her brow as the reality of what she'd done—was doing—hit her.

For the first time in forever she'd broken her own rule.

First she'd travelled alone with an unknown man. Now she was in a village where she didn't speak the dialect and her only back-up was Tom. A man she knew little about other than that he was a respected doctor.

She'd used all her street smarts to coerce him to bring her here, her need to do something for the children of Vietnam overriding the safety net she always cast about herself.

She hated the fact he'd correctly challenged her. She'd let her enthusiasm cloud her vision. How could she really help unless she truly understood the country? As much as she considered her inheritance 'tainted' money, she wanted to put it to good use. By the end of this trip she'd have a much clearer direction.

Since they'd left Hanoi, Tom had been polite, considerate and aloof. He'd arranged a lovely room for her when they'd overnighted in Lai Chau. Granted, it had been as far away from his as possible with a grove of trees between them, but that had suited her perfectly. Even at that distance he'd managed to feature in her dreams.

That morning Tom had introduced her to their interpreter, Hin, and with an appropriate professional manner and much bowing he'd made sure she'd been welcomed by the local health care worker.

She knew Tom really didn't want her here and merely tolerated her presence. Perhaps she'd allowed for a safety net after all.

'Drink?' Tom appeared behind her, offering her a bottle of water.

She turned and smiled, surprise snaking through her at his unexpected thoughtfulness. 'Thanks.' She twisted off the blue cap. 'Now, this sort of heat I can cope with. The humidity of the lowlands is almost too much for a girl from Perth.'

'At least you grew up in heat. Growing up on a dairy farm in the rainbelt of southern Victoria was no preparation at all.' He tipped his head back and gulped his drink down.

She tried to look away but her gaze was transfixed on the movement of his Adam's apple against his corded, muscular neck.

'That view's pretty amazing isn't it?'

She coughed, choking on her water while her cheeks flared with heat. Had he seen her blatant staring?

He swept his arm out at the panorama of green and grey mountains that ringed the village, their lower aspects carved and defined by terraces of emerald-green rice paddies. 'It looks so stunning and yet it makes life so damn hard for the locals.'

'Floods?' She'd seen debris, evidence that the Song Da River had in the past broken its banks.

'Floods and mudslides are one problem. The narrow valley means the river becomes a raging torrent and there's little room to escape. Add in the remoteness of the area, not being on a trade route and the government rightly cracking down on the opium-growing and it all means money is tight and so are ways to earn it.'

'What about tourism?' A thirst for knowledge gripped her.

'That's helped Lai Chau but it's only the really intrepid tourists that come out here.' He sighed. 'We even have trouble attracting local health workers. Sung, who you met when we arrived, could earn a lot more further south.'

'But she's here because she loves the place.'

His gaze intensified, as if he was really looking at her for the first time. 'How did you work that out so quickly?'

She shrugged, feeling slightly uncomfortable at his scrutiny and yet energised. This was the first sign he'd shown that he didn't think she was as flaky as his snap judgement had deemed her to be. 'You don't have to speak the language to understand. Observation is a telling tool.'

'True.' He recapped his water bottle.

'So what brought you here?' She'd wanted to ask that question since they'd met, but as he'd spent most of their travelling time listening to his MP3 player or avoiding her at the hotel, the opportunity hadn't arisen.

'Work.' The single word snapped out quickly. 'Are you ready for work?'

His abruptness startled her. 'Absolutely.'

He raised his brows. 'That's a favourite word of yours.'

'Is it? Have I used it before?'

He laughed, a deep, melodious sound that wrapped

around her like a blanket on a cold night, comforting and secure.

Scaring her down to her core.

No man had ever meant security in her world—only tyranny and fear. She created her own security. Keeping a distance from people meant keeping safe. She had no intention of changing.

His face became more serious. 'We're starting with a mother and baby clinic. You're on weighing and measuring babies. Then Sung can take you gardening. I hope you've got a green thumb. The home garden is one of the keys in battling child malnutrition.' He grinned, a wide smile, his almond-shaped eyes crinkling around the edges.

For the first time she caught a glimpse of Asia in his face, around his eyes and cheeks. *Nah, you're imagining that.* Surely people called him Dr Thông because that name was as close to Tom as the language allowed. A farm boy from Victoria, Dr Tom Bracken was as Aussie as they came.

He walked in front of her, his strong brown legs striding quickly over the short distance to the clinic. She suddenly realised he'd neatly steered the conversation away from himself. He hadn't answered her question at all.

A line of women dressed in colourful clothing snaked around the thatched clinic, their heads covered in fabric that looked strikingly similar to Scottish tartan. Long dresses of green, red, blue and black were covered in intricate embroidered patterns—a collage of colour.

Babies almost rigid from being overdressed, sat upright in their papooses, nestled against their mothers' backs.

The first time Tom had come to this region he'd thought he'd left Vietnam. The hill tribe minorities were very different from the coastal people and not much was familiar.

He glanced over at Bec, observing her reaction. Her tanned oval face was flushed with heat and loose strands of hair clung to her temples, glued there by sweat. But curiosity danced on her face, melding with respect as she bowed to the mothers, cooed to the babies and gently coaxed the toddlers away from their mothers' legs. And she achieved it all with hand signals and smiles.

She's done this before. Grudging admiration surfaced, which he quickly tempered. *It's early days.* 'Remember to use Hin.'

'Yes, Doctor.' Her eyes twinkled for an instant, their animation suddenly fading to match her almost blank expression. As if it was wrong to enjoy some light-hearted banter.

He couldn't work her out. For a woman who'd been so determined to come with him on this trip she'd been extremely tense around him. She was far more relaxed with the patients.

But he didn't have time to think about that. They were there to work. 'Any child who falls into the red zone when you put the mid upper arm circumference bracelet on them is cause for concern.'

She nodded, her face now serious, all traces of teasing gone. 'Right, I give them a swing in the weigh sling and I measure them on this.' She rolled out a bamboo mat and placed the measuring stick next to it.

'Any children needing supplemental feeding I'll keep here with their mothers. Between Hin, Sung and me, we'll have it sorted.' She washed her hands with quick-dry antibacterial solution. 'You'd better skedaddle and see the men.'

She'd just dismissed him. He tried to suppress the rising indignation sweeping through him. He should be pleased she was competent and he could get on with what he needed to do. Hell, he wasn't there to hold her hand.

He shook off the mantle of reluctance to leave her and headed over to greet the men.

Three hours later, drenched in sweat, and fighting visions of sliding into a clear, cool stream and lying under a waterfall, Bec examined her fiftieth child. She knew the stats about child malnutrition in Vietnam, and this village unfortunately skewed the average upwards.

And yet some children thrived. Were the families better off? Or did they just do things differently? She scribbled a note to herself. This was the sort of stuff she had to find out. She planned to question Sung closely when they went on their village vegetable garden tour. She had to maximise every moment of working there.

Her snap decision to come to the village was turning out to be the right thing after all. She hugged the knowledge to herself. It wasn't like she and Tom were spending any real time together anyway.

Tom had happily left her alone to run this clinic while he did his work. A plan rolled out in her head. They'd spend their days here involved in their own projects. She could work and learn, and still stick to her rule of keeping a safe distance. It was a win-win situation.

She glanced up to the next person in line. A woman stepped forward, her face impassive, carrying a toddler who lay limp and listless in her arms.

Dehydration. Bec's radar kicked in the moment she saw the sunken eyes in the child's small face. 'Hin, I need you. Can you, please, ask this mother how long her child has been sick and what the symptoms are?'

The interpreter, an easygoing young man in his twenties, spoke rapidly to the mother who responded and looked beseechingly at Bec as she sank to the ground, laying the child on the mat.

Bec knew why. This little girl was desperately ill. And she'd stake a bet the mother was pretty sick, too.

'She says the child has water coming from her bottom and she has been vomiting,' Hin succinctly translated.

'Has anyone else in the family been sick?'

More rapid-fire dialect spun around Bec. She desperately wished she could understand the words. But she *could* understand the emotions behind the words.

'This woman has been sick today. She has been vomiting and has had pains in her legs.'

'Tell her we can help.' Diarrhoea and vomiting were pretty common out here but Bec was worried by the complaint about pains in the legs.

Hin relayed Bec's words and then listened. 'She says many are sick. Some are here in the line, others are too sick to walk.'

Bec closed her eyes for a moment and breathed out

a long, slow breath. She touched the woman's shoulder reassuringly while her mind raced. 'Right. Hin, you go with Sung and talk to everyone who's waiting. Find out who has these symptoms and put those people together in another line.

'Ask if they have relatives who are sick as well. Draw a mud map of the village and mark on it every household that is sick. I'll be back in a minute.' She grabbed her hat and ran out of the hut toward the men's clinic. So much for working on her own.

'Tom!' She stood outside the hut and called, not wanting to barge into the clinic and undo the trust he'd built up.

He appeared almost immediately, smiling when he saw her. 'Finished already?'

She shook her head, ignoring the feeling in her gut his smile created. 'No, I think I'm just starting. I need your help.'

He raised his brows. 'Really? How so?'

She took no notice of the gentle jibe—she knew her independence and distance could sometimes grate in a team situation. 'I have a woman and child with severe dehydration.'

'That's pretty common, Bec. You'll need to mix up the oral rehydration solution.' A perplexed look crossed his face. 'I'm pretty sure I unpacked those boxes and stacked them in the women's hut when we arrived. Do you want me to look?'

Again, his thoughtfulness surprised her. She wasn't used to men acting like this. Not toward her, anyway. 'Thanks, but I know where the sachets are. My real concern is that this woman is complaining of diarrhoea, vomiting and leg cramps.'

His head snapped up, his dark eyes meeting hers. 'Does anyone else have the symptoms?'

She nodded slowly, knowing exactly where his mind was going. To the same conclusion she'd drawn. 'I've got Hin and Sung questioning the villagers. It sounds like cholera, doesn't it?'

'Damn it!' He ran his hands through his hair. 'Cholera's so contagious. It races through a community like wildfire. We need to set up a separate clinic, isolate all the affected people, start treatment and find the source.'

'As I have the first few patients in my hut, I guess we make that the isolation ward.' All thoughts of barrier nursing came pouring back into her head. 'Do we have chlorine to kill the bacterium?'

Worry lines scored his forehead. 'We do, but we also need it to wash their clothes. A laundry will have to be set up… I need to speak with the village elders.'

'Sung and I will get started on the makeshift quarantine area. I need to get the electrolyte solution into that child. I'll see you the moment you're back from meeting with the elders.' *Please, don't be too long.*

'Good plan. I'll be back as soon as I can.'

Did he read minds? 'Great.' She turned to go.

'Bec.' One syllable and yet it held both caution and concern.

She spun back to see his face filled with a mixture of authoritative control and unease.

'*Only* drink the bottled water from our supply and

only eat the food that Sung has prepared. I don't need you getting sick.'

A rush of emotion swirled inside her, battering the protective guard she'd erected long ago, frightening her.

Keep a safe distance.

She took in a deep breath and reinforced her guard. His caring tone, the worried look on his face didn't indicate concern for her. It was concern for the village. He needed all the help he could get to deal with this epidemic.

She tossed her head and flashed him her best 'don't boss me' look, similar to the one she'd used in Hanoi. The one that hid her true feelings. 'The same goes for you, too, Tom. I don't want to waste rehydration solution on someone who should have known better.'

She ran back to the clinic, thankful that the huge job in front of her wouldn't allow any time to think about a broad-shouldered, dark-haired doctor with deep worry lines between his chocolate-brown eyes. Lines she longed to smooth out.

'Tom, I'm sorry, but I think we need another IV.'

He glanced up from examining a woman whose eerie calm worried him intensely. She clung to life by a thread. In three days they hadn't lost a patient and he didn't want this woman to be their first.

Bec stood next to him, petite and exhausted from days of almost non-stop work. She should have been prostrate with fatigue but her strength and implacable determination kept her going.

She'd organised a remarkable clinic in a short space of time and with limited resources. Everyone who entered the isolation ward washed their hands and feet at the chlorine station beside the door.

Patients lay on bamboo mats with one member of their family to care for them. Bec had organised the healthy men into a team to dig a new latrine and the area around the clinic had been quarantined with a fence. Fires burned continuously outside, boiling water to make it potable. Further away, women boiled the clothes of the sick.

'We've got plenty of oral solution but intravenous packs are getting low.' She worried at her bottom lip with her top teeth.

His blood surged.

Fury at himself immediately followed. What the hell was wrong with him? Vomiting patients surrounded him, he was cloaked in heat, operating in the most basic of medical facilities, and now his body was reacting like a hormone-fuelled teenager's.

Bec was a nurse, a much-needed colleague, nothing more.

Make that your mantra. 'If we have a patient who needs an IV, we insert it. And we hope the new supplies arrive before we run out.' He rose slowly, weariness vibrating through him.

'Can you insert the IV now, please? Then you need to take a break.' Clear, violet-blue eyes bored through him.

Indignation bristled. 'You should talk. You've been going for longer than me. I get to sit down when I do my daily briefings with the elders. So I'll insert the IV, you do another oral rehydration round and then we'll *both* take a break.'

She held his gaze, her mouth firm. Suddenly, the corners twitched upwards and she smiled. 'Fair enough. But only because the local health worker from the next village has arrived to help.'

Her smile took away the tension that seemed to dog her.

He couldn't help grinning back. 'Deal.'

Hin explained to the mother of the child about inserting the IV and Bec held both the mother's and the child's hands. Tom continued to be amazed at how she seemed to channel supportive care and understanding to these women and children.

Somehow he managed to slide the cannula into the almost collapsed veins of the dehydrated child. As he reached to release the tourniquet, Bec moved forward to tape the needle securely to the skin.

Their hands collided, his palm gently skating over her fingers.

She flinched, her hand suddenly rigid, hovering over the child's arm. Tension vibrated up her arm and through her body. A moment stretched out, her hand suspended, fingers taut.

He glanced at her as he released the tourniquet. Her colour, usually tanned and healthy, had faded to ivory. Her skin stretched tightly across her high cheekbones.

She moved jerkily, her fingers flexing before she quickly taped the drip in place. 'I can't believe how effective the oral rehydration solution is. I would have thought antibiotics would have been required.' The words had rushed out, tumbling over each other.

Her reaction to an accidental touch mystified him completely. But an inexplicable need to protect her surged inside him. He matched her conversation, hoping to put her at ease. 'It's amazing what some salt water, sugar, potassium, magnesium and other electrolytes can do.'

He ran his hand through his hair. 'Although it's the glucose that does the trick. It means the sodium moves into the gut, taking the electrolytes and fluid with it, and that's the key to rehydration. Simple yet so effective and life saving.'

'Talking simple but effective, I can smell the rice soup Sung's made for us.' Bec stood up, her usual 'in-control' demeanour back in place. 'Let's go.' She waited for him to start walking, as if she didn't trust he would follow her.

'We need a complete break so how about we eat outside?' He led the way, hearing her gentle, uneven footsteps behind him, her slight limp more audible than noticeable.

They sat under the shade of a tree, clutching their bowls of rice soup as reverently as if they were highly coveted and rare French truffles.

Bec had chosen a position that left a good metre between them. He noticed she did that a lot. In the truck coming up she'd sat so close to the door that if she'd been any closer she would have been outside the vehicle. And the flinching thing when they'd inserted the drip. What had that been about?

If she feared him, why had she insisted on coming here with him? A guarded reserve and general aloofness toward him seemed to clash at times with real care and concern. But with the women and children she lost that tenseness. He couldn't work her out.

She put her bowl down. 'So we're winning, right? Today we've only had five new cases?'

'We have. This time. But until we can find out a way to truly make a change in a tradition, this sort of outbreak will continue.'

'What do you mean?' Her eyes sparked with genuine interest. He could almost see her brain ticking over.

'Human excreta fertiliser.'

'Really?'

He smiled at her dumbfounded look. 'The government is making headway by using the local area health workers, but it's a long, slow haul, especially in remote communities like this. This practice dates back centuries and the beliefs about it bringing good crops are well entrenched.'

'And they only get one crop a year…' Her voice trailed away.

She understood. A warm glow burned inside him. 'That's right. Plus we're close to the border with China here and sometimes cholera comes in that way. But no outbreaks have been reported up there so I think this outbreak must have been started with unwashed vegetables and then it was propelled and promoted by a lack of handwashing and food-preparation skills.'

Bec pulled a crumpled piece of paper out of her pocket and smoothed it on her knee. 'This is a copy of the mud map of the village. Most of the cases came from this area.' She pointed with her finger.

His gaze fixed on her fine, tapered fingers as he moved toward her to study the diagram.

A line of tension ran through her but she didn't move

away. 'Why did this section of the village get sick and the other areas didn't?'

'We could surmise that they used the fertiliser.'

'True, but this is also the area where there is the most malnutrition.' She turned toward him, almost vibrating with excitement. 'Families all live together or very close to each other so we could conclude that what some extended families do in their daily life can seem to guard them against illness, whereas the practices of other families lead to illness and malnutrition for their children.'

Her energy encased him. 'So what are you saying?'

Enthusiasm glowed on her face. 'What if we get the women in the village to identify which women and children are not malnourished? If they can make the connection that some families are eating well and are not often sick then surely they will want to find out how.'

Exhilaration swept through him at her insight. 'So instead of us teaching a new way of doing things, the villagers discover it and change the way they have been doing things, based on a positive role model.'

She tilted her head. 'Yes and no. We foster the change by setting up opportunities like your gardens. We use positive role models and the health care workers.' She wrinkled her nose in thought. 'Perhaps cooking classes but they gather the food first... I don't know, I'm making it up as I go along.'

He gazed at her, stunned at what she'd just come up with.

'I think I owe you an apology.'

Lines scored her brow. 'Why?'

'When I met you in Hanoi and you seemed so vague about what you wanted to do, how you wanted to help, I thought…'

'You thought I was flaky.'

Her matter-of-fact tone slugged him. 'Sorry.'

She shrugged. 'You had a valid point. I was vague. I do want to fix it all. You've forced me to focus. I wanted to rush in and now I see that I need to take my time and work out what I want to do, how I can best help.'

He shot her a glance. 'Or how you're going to generate funds to do it.'

She sipped her tea. 'Oh, I've got the money, that isn't the problem.'

Her naïvety both entranced and frustrated him. 'It's going to take more than a few thousand dollars to start up a clinic.'

'Will two hundred and fifty thousand dollars do it?'

He choked on his tea. 'You have a quarter of a million dollars at your disposal?'

She grimaced, her expression unexpectedly hard. 'I do.'

Her expression worried him. 'Are you certain you want to use all of it in aid? I mean, I assume you've allowed enough for your own needs.'

'I won't have *anything* to do with that money.' The words, almost menacing, rolled out on a low growl. 'It needs to work off its origins and do some good in the world. Every child deserves a childhood so they can grow up to be a productive adult. This money will help them achieve that.'

She stood up abruptly. 'We need to get back.'

Before he could start to ask even one of the numerous questions that had slammed into his mind, she'd turned and marched off toward the clinic, her hair tumbling out of its restrictive band, softening the rigid line of her shoulders.

Part of him wanted to go to her and let his fingers caress the tension from her shoulders, entwine with the softness of her hair…

Stop it. It was official—sleep deprivation had finally got to him. Massaging her shoulders—it was an insane thought. Besides, she'd hate it. Hell, she'd shuddered when his hand had accidentally touched hers.

Getting involved with a woman wasn't an option. He'd made that decision after two failed relationships. Both women had demanded his full attention. He couldn't offer anyone that until he'd sorted out his own life. Filled in the missing gaps. So why was he wasting time, thinking like this?

Because she intrigues you like no one else ever has.

He tried to push the voice away, empty his thoughts but Bec's voice whooshed in. *I won't have anything to do with that money.*

That statement generated more questions than answers.

He sighed. He hadn't wanted her to come on this trip but instead of carrying her, as he'd expected he'd have to, she'd proved her worth in a thousand ways.

But the more time he spent with her the more he needed to know about her. She was a bundle of contradictions. What lay behind her determination to work here? He'd stake his life it wasn't just a philanthropic desire.

Tom understood that well. For years he'd ignored the call of Vietnam. He was Australian. And yet he was

Vietnamese. He had Australian parents who loved him. But their DNA wasn't part of him. And Vietnam continued to call to that empty space inside him that craved answers.

He pushed himself to his feet. He was working with the best nurse he'd ever met. That was *all* he needed to know about her. Nothing else mattered. Everyone had their own journey and he needed to focus on his. He didn't need to get involved in hers.

They were colleagues—pure and simple.

CHAPTER THREE

BEC SCOOPED WATER over herself, savouring the sensation of the cool liquid sluicing in rivulets across her heat-irritated skin. As she tipped water from the bamboo cup along her arm, she fantasised about continuous water flowing from a shower nozzle.

But her fantasy was as close as she was going to get. The villagers bathed in the river but she had a strong suspicion that she'd get out of the silt-filled water feeling grimier than when she'd got in. She laughed ruefully that her definition of luxury had been reduced to using some of her meagre supplies of her favourite shampoo.

Her frenetic workload had finally eased. New medical supplies had arrived to replenish the dwindling stocks and no new cases of cholera had appeared. For seven days and nights she'd worked flat out, grabbing power sleeps when she could.

Just like Tom.

Tom.

She dumped water over her head to wash out the shampoo. To wash out the image of a doctor whose delicious lopsided grin seemed to radiate shafts of sunlight and send tendrils of warmth right down to the dark recesses of her soul. A smile that generated such a need in her that it scared her rigid.

She'd be in the middle of an observation round and find herself deliberately searching for him, glancing around until she found him.

On the few occasions he'd caught her glance he'd smiled. Sometimes a broad smile, other times a quirky grin. A 'How's it going?' smile. A 'You doing OK?' smile. And she found herself wanting and needing to see that smile again.

For the first time in her life she had a glaring insight into the trials of someone trying to give up something addictive like cigarettes. She'd *tried* not to look, but she was fighting a losing battle. She craved his smile.

The knowledge terrified her.

She'd come on this trip to learn about Vietnam's health needs, *not* to learn about Tom. But for every time she told herself to focus on her job, a new question about Tom flashed into her head, piling itself on top of the growing list.

Why was he here? What was his connection with Vietnam? In some lights the shape of his wide eyes could be considered Asian but nothing else about him was faintly oriental. He was far from fluent in Vietnamese but his way with the patients showed an innate understanding. The questions went round and round in her head.

She grabbed her micro-fibre towel and started vigorously rubbing her skin dry. These strange and unsettling feelings must be connected to being plunged into a foreign and unfamiliar culture, and being surrounded by a language of which she had minimal understanding. Tom, with his laconic Australian approach to life, was the only thing familiar. Of course she would seek him out. It was only a natural extension of being here and feeling a bit displaced.

It had nothing to do with attraction or need. She did *not* need a man in her life.

She jerkily pulled on her clothes, jammed her hat on her head and strode toward the clinic. Not that she needed to be there now the crisis had eased. She knew she should be taking a break while she had the chance, but she was restless and agitated.

She poured a bucket of hot water from the big pot above the fire and hauled it up the steps. Keeping busy had worked for her all her life. When things got tough, she worked. There was no reason why that strategy wouldn't keep being useful.

She sloshed water onto the floor and knelt down, attacking the boards with a brush. Tom had mentioned a meeting with the village elders so she'd take advantage of his absence and scrub the clinic.

'What are you doing?'

She glanced up from her position on the floor, scrubbing brush poised in mid-air. Her breath stalled, catching in her throat.

Tom leant casually against the doorframe, his bulk making the bamboo casing look very flimsy. A clean, pressed T-shirt outlined his chest and arms, his biceps pushing the fabric to full stretch. Beads of water hung from the curling tips of his black hair and his skin almost sparkled, completely devoid of the grime of village life.

Clean, fresh, wholesome and incredibly sexy.

A surge of heat, carried on a wave of wonder raced through every part of her, awakening areas that had been dormant for too long.

He strode forward and removed the brush from her hand, setting it down on a table behind him. 'Today we rest.'

She stood up, stretching her arm out for the brush, desperately trying to recover her composure. She spoke without thinking. 'Who made you the boss?'

He threw his head back and laughed, the muscles of his neck rippling with mirth. 'Ah, I believe Health For Life, and you did agree in Hanoi I was in charge.'

'Well, sure, when it comes to patients.' She stuck her hand on her hip, trying to show a cool detachment she didn't feel. 'But no doctor ever dares to interfere with nurses and their cleaning. That is our domain. Florence Nightingale mandated it.'

He shrugged. 'Perhaps I'm feeling brave today.' He put on a mock-serious tone. 'As the medical officer in charge of this operation I'm invoking section 47 B, schedule 9 of the work charter. That means no cleaning today, Bec.' A teasing grin danced on his lips.

Her legs suddenly wobbled. She locked her knees for support. 'You're making that up.'

'Only the bit about schedule 9.' His teasing grin faded, replaced by a serious expression. 'Yesterday the health workers had a rest day. With no new cases of cholera it's our turn to take a break. We're no use to anyone if we fall over from fatigue.' His intense gaze zeroed in on her. 'Are we, Bec?'

She shifted uneasily, feeling like a rabbit caught in headlights. 'I suppose.' To her horror she sounded like a petulant four-year-old. Part of her knew he was right but the other part wanted to bury herself in the safety of work.

'Excellent. Glad you agree with me.' His brows rose wickedly.

Was he flirting with her? Ribbons of excitement spread through her, both delicious and terrifying. She immediately squashed the unwanted emotions. Men couldn't be trusted. She would never fall for dark eyes and pretty words again.

She tossed her head. 'As you've banned me from work I will go and…' Her brain blanked. She struggled to think of something to do. She tossed her head. 'Read my book.'

Tom folded his arms across his chest. 'I get the feeling I can't trust you not to scrub every surface of this clinic. I'm taking you to the Sunday market in a village about an hour's drive away, up by the Chinese border.' He smiled. 'You need to see Vietnam's diversity. Consider it part of your research.'

A day out alone with Tom. Fear collided with desire, tumbling over and over in the pit of her stomach. 'That's a kind offer but really you don't have to. I promise I won't come near the clinic and—'

'You're babbling and you're coming with me.'

Something in his matter-of-fact tone propelled her to the door and outside. She was being childish and he was trying to be helpful and kind.

Where was the harm? She'd spend the day wandering around the market surrounded by crowds. She'd still be able to keep her safe distance both physically and emotionally. 'Thanks. It sounds like fun.' She started to walk toward the four-wheel-drive.

'Bec.'

She spun around.

'The road's too narrow for the truck.' Tom stood next to a motorbike, extending a helmet toward her.

Her blood rushed to her feet, making her sway. Panic trickled through her, intensifying as it spread. Spending a day alone with Tom at a market full of people was one thing. Sitting behind him on a motorbike, with millimetres between them, was another.

Her need for a safe distance intensified.

Any ideas of exactly how to achieve it diminished fast.

Tom brought the motorbike to a halt and turned the ignition off. Before the sound of the engine had died away, Bec quickly hopped off the bike, her actions almost frantic. She had to be the most tense passenger he'd ever transported. She'd sat, completely rigid, the entire trip.

She pulled off her helmet, and her hair fell down, framing her unusually pale face.

'You OK?' Concern for her ricocheted through him.

She took in a deep breath. 'Those last few bends were pretty wild.'

'Sorry. You fought the curves and got motion sickness. You need to be at one with them and at one with the bike. On the way home, lean into them.'

Lean into me and relax. The disquieting thought thundered through him.

Her eyes widened, darkening to an inky blue. A flicker of something vibrated in their depths and faded as quickly as it had appeared. 'What's in this box that was so important that I had to have it stick into me for the last hour?' An unusual huskiness clung to her voice.

He released the elastic straps, which had held the box in place during the bumpy journey. 'Condoms.'

'You've come to a local market with four hundred condoms?' She started to giggle. 'I had no idea they were legal tender. Here I was thinking it was the dong.'

He laughed with her, appreciating her quick wit, enchanted by how her face changed when she completely relaxed. The stress lines around her eyes and mouth faded, her cheeks softened and her eyes danced. Lazy heat spread through him.

'Cheeky.' He lifted the box and started walking up the hill to a small cement building.

She quickly caught up with him despite her limp. 'I thought you said it was a no-work day, that we needed a break.' Her expression challenged him.

'We do, but seeing as we're in the area I'm just dropping off some gear at the clinic.'

She shook her head in disbelief. 'Talk about the pot calling the kettle black. You're as bad as I am for not turning off.'

He met her gaze and grinned. 'No one is as bad as you for not turning off.'

'Hey.' She playfully elbowed him gently in the ribs, her face alive with fun.

The moment she'd done it she flinched, her body stiffening as if she'd received an electric shock. Her arm shot back to her side and regret tinged with fear scored her face. Immediately, she stepped away, putting a large space between them.

Again.

Her shocked expression surprised him. Hell, what did she think he would do to her? The idea that she thought he might hurt her, that he wouldn't know her action was part of a joke, sliced through him like a razor, leaving a dull, throbbing ache in its wake.

She stepped slightly ahead of him.

He caught up in two long strides. 'Seeing as we're in the area, I'm just killing two birds with one stone.'

'As will the condoms.' She fanned herself with her hat as they reached the clinic and stepped into the shade.

Respect for her insight swirled through him. 'That's right. Condoms for family planning and to help stop the spread of HIV. It's a problem all over the country but up here with the opium trade and the illegal trade of women back and forth across the border, it's worse.'

'So whenever you're in the area you make sure the health workers are well supplied.'

He nodded as he turned his back to her, putting the box down next to a large poster about HIV. He ripped off the duct tape.

'You're a good man, Tom Bracken.'

He shouldn't have heard the softly whispered words over the noise of tape coming off the cardboard. Words tinged with wonder. The unexpected, almost secret compliment stroked him like a soft caress. Warming him.

Completely puzzling him.

He'd never met a woman like her. She was kind,

caring and generous with her time, her skills and money. Professionally, she was always in control and yet out of the work environment she lurched from open and fun to completely closed up, verging on timid and fearful.

She was a bundle of contradictions. What had made her like this?

His need to know intensified. He had to find out, and he would. He just had to choose his moment. He stood up and turned around to face her.

She met his gaze with her hands on her hips, eyebrows arched and a slight sardonic twinge to her mouth.

Now wasn't the time.

'So, you promised me a market tour.' The in-control, assertive Bec was back.

'You're right, I did. Let's go shopping.'

Bec gently fingered the brightly coloured motif. For the last hour she'd lost herself in the buzz and hum of the market, letting the crowd jostle around her, listening to the calls of 'You buy' and 'Come my stall.' Letting all of it push the mess of thoughts out of her head.

All thoughts of Tom.

She needed to think of him in terms of a doctor and a humanitarian aid worker. Not a man. She gave herself an internal shake. What was wrong with her? Usually, she could resist men. For eight years she'd had no problem resisting men. No problem at all.

But when Tom's heat had radiated into her body on the motorbike all her hard-fought resolve had taken a pounding.

She ran her finger over a piece of intricate embroidery, the vivid colours of red, green and blue woven closely together.

'It's amazing, isn't it?' Tom appeared by her side, having wandered behind her as if he knew she wanted to be alone for a while. 'The Dzao women are incredibly skilled at this needlework.' He turned to the hovering woman who owned the rickety stall and asked her a question in Vietnamese.

The woman answered, her words rapid. She put her hand on Bec's arm. 'You, come.'

Bec glanced at Tom for confirmation, wondering what he had asked her.

He nodded for her to follow the woman. 'She's going to show us how they make the thread and stitch the designs.'

'Fantastic.' She followed the woman a short distance where pots of boiling water contained fabric and women stirred the contents with big wooden sticks.

'They buy the raw silk at the markets and boil it to make it smooth. Then they dye it using natural dye from plants like tea and turmeric.' He picked up the distinctive yellow turmeric. 'The colours represent their ancestors who they worship.'

'The designs are so interesting. What's that?' She pointed to a motif.

Tom peered at it. 'Gibbon hands. They use all sorts of things to inspire their designs, even food.' His long fingers pointed out cabbages.

The woman shoved a large square into Bec's hands, covered in intricate stitches. Then she turned and patted her own bottom. *'Luy khia.'*

Bec looked beseechingly at Tom. 'What's this for?'

He grinned. 'It's the lower flap of a jacket. I think she wants to dress you like the Dzao. The trousers are actually strips of fabric wrapped around the legs and decorated with stripes of colour.' His deep voice rumbled around her, solid, reliable and informative.

'How do you know so much?' Most men didn't know anything about women's clothing.

He shrugged his shoulders in an almost overly casual way. 'I guess I was interested and as my language improved I asked questions.'

'Did you learn Vietnamese on the dairy farm?' She threw the question out, her tone informal, trying to hide how much she craved to learn more about him.

A momentary shadow crossed his face, immediately replaced by a lightness that softened his expression. The two conflicting emotions puzzled her.

'Not much call for Vietnamese in Gippsland.' His laugh, normally deep and warm, sounded shallow. 'That flap of embroidery you're holding goes at the base of the jacket. Then there's a belt to hold the flap up out of the rice when you're working in the fields.'

'Sounds complicated.' She glanced at him. Damn it, if he hadn't done it again and changed the subject.

His open expression denied any sign he was actively avoiding answering her question. 'That's only part of it. Their headdress is a triangular-shaped turban decorated with silver coins.' He moved closer to her, showing her the silver decorations stitched to the fabric.

'The wealth of a woman is measured by the weight

of the coins carried in her costume.' He gave her a sly look. 'Your headdress would be heavy indeed.'

She ignored his comment, not wanting to think about her father or his money. 'Perhaps I could buy one of those?' She picked up a tasselled shoulder bag.

'Good idea. You could use it to hold all those other knick-knacks you bought. There's no pannier on the bike.'

The motorbike. How could she have forgotten *that*?

With much serious head-nodding and hand-wringing Bec went through the bargaining process. She'd have been happy to hand over the first price asked but then everyone would lose face.

Thrilled with her purchase, she slung the bag over her shoulder and turned to Tom. 'How does it look?'

His eyes gazed appreciatively at her. 'Totally gorgeous.'

Heat flared inside her, whipping through her and racing across her cheeks like a grass fire. She wasn't used to this. Men didn't look at her like that.

Nick had.

Reality doused her, a chill creeping through her. The stars in her eyes had blinded her to signs of the cold, calculating man he was.

'Bec?'

She heard Tom's voice and realised she was gripping the handle of the bag so tightly her knuckles were white. 'Sorry, what did you say?'

'It's time to head back.' Tom tilted his head back up the road.

Five minutes later she climbed onto the bike, her bottom as far back on the seat as possible, her hands gripping the metal bar of the package rack behind her.

The bike roared into life and Tom cautiously wove through the crowd as they made their way out of town. He headed off the main road onto a track which climbed steeply.

The bike shuddered as it hit a deep pothole.

A silent scream exploded in Bec's chest. She flung her arms around his waist and threw her body against his back as visions of being splattered against an unforgiving baked clay road came into her head. She buried her face in his shoulder, closing her eyes, and tried to think calm thoughts.

The bike bounced again.

Where was that image of a waterfall when she needed it? Terror roared in her ears. She tried to breathe in and out slowly, focusing on the breath.

The firmness of Tom's back against her chest was soothing as his warmth trickled through her. Her breaths came more easily.

Like spring sunshine after a long winter, his heat gently warmed her, calming her, bringing a languid peace. She relaxed against him, the contours of her breasts and belly moulding to the muscles and sinew of his back.

The bike steadied.

You can let go now, the scary bit's over. The cotton of his shirt softly caressed her cheek.

The bike took a curve, leaning into the bend. *I need to lean into the curves to avoid motion sickness.*

You need to keep a safe distance.

She hummed a song to herself, blocking out the argument in her head. This was transportation. Nothing else.

Bend after bend, curve upon curve, she swayed with Tom and the bike, keeping her eyes closed, drinking in the sensation of heat, wind and motion. Holding reality at bay.

The bike slowed to a crawl.

Disappointment rammed through her and reality jolted back into place. She dropped her arms from Tom's waist, resting them on her knees.

He brought the bike to a halt, kicked out the stand and hopped off. 'Sorry about the rough patch, but I wanted you to see this.'

Pulling off her helmet, she followed the sweep of his arm. She gasped. 'I had no idea. I had my eyes closed most of the time.'

Tom laughed. 'I thought you might have, but the view's worth a few bumps, isn't it?'

She stood up and turned slowly. Everywhere she looked towering mountains dominated, a stunning mixture of red earth, green trees and grey scree. Way below them a river wound its way through the mountains and in the distance a tiny village perched precariously on a ridge, with crops clinging to a steep face. 'It's amazing. It's like being on the top of the world.'

He nodded, a smile of understanding rippling across his face. 'Beyond those mountains is China.'

'Really? Vietnam shares so many borders. It's mind-boggling for a girl from a big island.' Walking slowly, she approached the cliff edge. 'It always stuns me to think that water can carve out such a mighty gorge.' She stepped forward wanting a closer look, to peer way down at the river below.

As her foot touched the ground, an agonising cramp

gripped her left leg. Shafts of pain radiated into every muscle and tendon. She gasped, throwing her arms out to steady herself as her leg collapsed under her.

'Careful.' Tom's hands grabbed her, pulling her to his side as he eased her down to the ground. 'I don't want to lose you over the edge.'

Her heart pounded, adrenaline meshing with fear. 'Thanks. That could have been nasty.'

A questioning look mixed with concern radiated from his eyes. 'Let's look at that leg. It seems to bother you quite a bit.'

'It's fine, really.' She tried to pull her leg up toward her chest, away from him. A spasm spiralled from hip to toe, clenching every muscle. She bit her lip against the blinding pain.

'It's not OK at all.' He pushed the sole of her shoe up, flexing the foot against the cramp.

Red-hot pain shot through her, slowly easing as the counter-pressure wove its magic. Her shoulders slumped as the pain receded. 'That's better, thank you.'

She expected him to release her foot but instead his hand brushed the cotton of her trousers up to her knee. He laid his fingers against her skin, gently kneading her calf, slowly unbunching the knots of tangled muscles.

Rockets of delicious sensation streaked through her. A pulse point fluttered in her neck, fire burned in her belly. His hands on her skin sent waves of longing lapping against her reinforced defences.

You know not to trust a man. Keep a safe distance.

Panic surged. 'You really don't have to do that, I'm

fine now.' She tried to pull the leg of her trousers back down over her lower leg.

He raised his dark brows as his hands stilled on her leg. 'My fingers are telling me otherwise, Bec. I notice you limp and obviously the extra strain of being on your feet for days has taken its toll.' His finger traced a long red scar down her leg. 'What happened to you?'

The locked memory creaked open. She forced it closed. 'I broke my leg.' She tugged the cotton against his hands. *Please, don't go there.*

'It must have been a nasty break to leave you with some shortening and a limp.' His expression was neutral but his eyes burned with determination to find out more.

Buried memories bubbled inside her, their pain always snagging her at unexpected moments, dragging her down to the sordid mess that had been her childhood.

She didn't want to go back there.

She stared into his eyes. Genuine caring reflected back to her, coupled with resolve. He wouldn't let it go, he'd keep at her until she told him. If she refused to open up to him now she'd only be putting off the inevitable.

She drew her legs up to her chest, hugging her arms tightly around her knees, wrapping herself in a protective layer to withstand the inevitable resurgence of pain. 'My father pushed me down a flight of stairs, fracturing every bone in my leg.'

CHAPTER FOUR

TOM'S BREATH SHUDDERED out of his lungs as an image of Bec, sprawled on the ground in pain, thundered through him.

Of all the scenarios he'd run through his head, that had *not* been one of them. The aura of fragility he'd occasionally glimpsed swirled around her, then vanished with a stiffening of her shoulders.

It was as if she was rising through her pain. Her courage awed him.

She lightened her grim expression with a wry smile. 'Bet you weren't expecting that explanation.'

He should have anticipated this ironic reaction from her—facing the facts head on, deflecting any sympathy. He had a sudden urge to hold her close, wanting to hug her, but every ounce of her petite frame screamed, *Do not touch*.

So he stuck with the facts. 'You're right, I was thinking more along the lines of a car accident or being thrown off a horse. How old were you?'

She took in a deep breath. 'Sixteen and sassy. Sixteen, naïve and stupid.'

He hated the way she implied that part of what had happened had been her fault. 'All of us are naïve at sixteen, Bec.'

She shook her head. 'I should have known better. Anger had been part of my life for as long as I could remember. My father's rages were legendary. My mother protected me, taking the brunt of his fists to keep me safe, but eventually he wore her down and wore her out. She committed suicide when I was thirteen.' Her flat voice delivered the words, devoid of any emotion. Only her white knuckles betrayed her pain.

The image of his father's weather-beaten face, creased with a laconic grin, flooded Tom's mind. He'd only ever known love from his adoptive father. The only father he could remember.

White rage burned inside him, hot yet impotent, uselessly directed at a faceless man who had caused so much pain. 'So you lost your mother and your buffer?'

She nodded. 'But I quickly worked out that if I studied hard at school, agreed with most of what he said and retreated into the background of his life, I could get away with being screamed at rather than hit.'

Deep inside him an aching pain twisted. 'Until you grew into a woman.'

Her violet eyes darkened to indigo as her brow creased in surprise. 'Is that what changed?'

He sighed. 'I met men like your father during my psychiatric rotation. They have a pathological hatred of women. Once their daughter grows up they see that normal development as a betrayal of their love.' He hated how trite the theory sounded against Bec's reality.

She shrugged. 'Whatever. All I know is that things got pretty bad and I had to leave home for my own safety. Only I mistimed my departure and he arrived home to find me with my bags packed.' A flinching shudder vibrated through her body.

The same shudder he'd seen when his hand had accidentally brushed hers at the clinic. The same flinch as earlier that day at the market, moments after she'd playfully elbowed him. Hell, all this time she'd been on alert, ready to dodge and duck, thinking he might hurt her.

Nausea rolled in his stomach. He wanted to flatten the lowlife who'd created this fear within her. He wanted to make things better but rationally he knew he couldn't. Yet he had to try. 'You don't have to relive this if you don't want to.'

Her mouth firmed and her chin jutted. 'A half-told story is as bad as a suppressed one. Surely you learned that in your psych rotation?' Her eyes flashed with pain and resentment.

His heart took a direct hit with her jibe. 'I apologise. I ignored your signals that you didn't want to talk, I asked you a question and I've pushed for an answer. You're right, now I need to listen.'

She blinked. Twice. A look of incredulity raced across her face as if she didn't believe what she'd just heard. She cleared her throat. 'To cut a long story short, after I refused to return to my room he threw my bags down the stairs. Then he threw me. In a way it got me out of his life for good. Child Protection stepped in and court orders prevented him from making any contact.'

His gut ached for her but he knew she didn't want sympathy. 'At sixteen, though, you were still a kid. Where did you live?'

For the first time in a long time she smiled at a memory. 'With my aunt—my mother's sister. *He'd* not allowed contact with any family so at least that gave me the chance to get to know my real family.'

My real family. He chased away the thoughts her words generated in him. His real family, the one he hadn't been able to find. Yet.

'Hey, don't look so pensive on my account. I got out. Some kids don't.' Her pretty face took on a hard edge.

He recognised that expression. He'd seen it cross her face once before. The time she'd talked about the money she had for the clinic. *I won't have anything to do with that money.*

'That two hundred and fifty thousand dollars you want to use for children—it's your father's money, isn't it?'

She bit her lip and nodded slightly. 'He left it to me in his will. It was the only paternal thing he ever did. You don't miss much, do you?' She stared at him, the look long and intense.

A look that saw through him, carving deeply, all the way down to the essence of his soul. His gut, which had ached in pain for her, suddenly lurched. Unexpected longing poured through him. What would it be like to have those eyes gaze at him without their shadows?

The thought shocked him. He fought to clear his mind, stay fixed on her story. 'I guess putting the pieces of a puzzle together are part of my job. After all, that's what diagnosis is.'

'I guess it is.' She trailed some fine gravel through her hand.

He spoke to her bowed head. 'I understand now why you don't want to use any of that money for yourself.'

Her eyes glittered hard and sharp for a moment. 'He will not buy me from the grave.' A softer expression wafted across her face. 'But I will use his money to work for the greater good.'

Everything fell into place. 'And that's why you want to use the money to improve children's lives?' He stood up and stretched his hands out, pulling her to her feet.

She rose up toward him, nodding so vehemently that her hair slipped out of its band. 'Every child deserves a childhood. Without a childhood how can they grow to adulthood and take on a productive place in society?

'They need a guarantee of their basic human rights, to live without fear, to have access to food and clean water, health care and education.' She looked up at him, her sparkling eyes a stunning shade of iris blue. Her lithe body pulsed with the passionate conviction of her beliefs.

His blood heated, surging through his body and pooling in his groin. Her passion and fervour set off a chain reaction, bringing alive every nerve ending in his body, sensation stacking on sensation, driving down to the tips of his toes.

He knew he should let go of her hands but he wanted to soak up her enthusiasm, her innate goodness. His thumbs stroked the backs of her hands, the gentle circular motion absorbing her heat, sucking in her energy, trying to claim a part of her for himself.

Her eyes widened, two translucent discs unfettered by shutters, barriers and guards.

He thought he glimpsed a woman's naked need, a flare of desire.

For an infinitesimal moment she swayed toward him.

He recognised the precise moment she stopped herself.

Regret surged through him. His arms ached to hold her, to feel her body moulded against his own, just like on the ride up the mountain. He wanted to feel her face snuggled against his shoulder, wanted to let his head drop down against her silky hair and lose himself in her distinctively fresh scent of cinnamon apples. Wanted to taste her, feel her soft lips yielding against his own.

It scared the hell out of him.

He specialised in detachment. He didn't get involved with anyone. Never had. He couldn't offer a woman anything until he'd found the missing piece of himself. And Bec didn't want his touch.

So why did the thought of changing the rules even enter his head?

'Leprosy?' Bec couldn't believe what she was hearing. 'There's leprosy in this country?'

She and Tom were pulling medical kits out of the back of a truck. They'd left the far northwest of the country yesterday after three weeks in the village. She hadn't wanted to leave.

She'd never worked so hard in her life as she had during the cholera outbreak. Amidst the hard work and heartache she'd fallen in love with the tenacity of the villagers and the glorious mountains that isolated them.

She'd learnt more in three weeks than in all her years at university.

Now they were on the coast. Wide sandy beaches edged with tall coconut trees extended both north and south as far as the eye could see.

'There's still some leprosy, although we're winning and the rates have dropped dramatically. According to the World Health Organization we're pretty close to eliminating the disease. But the stigma causes social problems and the health of the lepers needs constant monitoring.' He handed her a medical kit backpack and smiled. A restrained smile.

She swallowed a sigh. She missed the wide, cheeky grin he used to give her and still gave everyone else. She hadn't been the recipient of that smile since their trip to the Sunday market.

When he'd stood so close to her at the lookout, holding her hands and caressing her skin with his thumbs, coils of yearning had unravelled inside her like silk streaming in the wind. Glorious sensations had spread through her, making her knees buckle. She'd desperately wanted to lean into him. Wanted to rest her body against him and snuggle into the shelter of his arms.

But stepping into his arms would have been a huge mistake. Way too big a risk.

So she'd pulled back and a dull pain had started to throb under her ribs. It had never completely left her.

When he'd released her hands his eyes had flickered with an emotion she hadn't quite been able to pin down. Probably relief. The last thing he needed was an emotional nurse throwing herself into his arms. Now he seemed almost wary around her. She missed the laid-back doctor she'd first met.

She straightened her shoulders. None of that mattered. What mattered was the time she had left to learn all she could from him about Vietnam. Then she could decide the best way she could help the children of this wonderful country.

'Follow me down to the boat.' Tom turned and walked across the sand.

Bec scanned the water, looking for a boat, but she could only see gentle waves and the horizon. Five fishermen sat on the beach mending nets, leaning up against enormous round bamboo baskets.

As they approached, one of the men rose and greeted Tom. He turned over the large basket and floated it in the water.

'Put your pack in the middle and then hop in.' Tom gently placed his pack on the floor of the eight-foot-diameter basket.

Bec shrugged her pack off her shoulders. 'Where's the boat?'

Tom laughed, his eyes dancing. 'This is it.'

Her shriek of surprise caused a great deal of mirth amongst the fishermen. 'This is a boat?'

'It's a Vietnamese dinghy, a basket boat. It's made from woven bamboo and covered in a waterproof tar-like substance, which is actually sap from a tree. It gets me safely to the island every time I visit.'

He caught her gaze, his eyes suddenly intense and earnest. 'Trust me, Bec.' He held out his hand.

Trust me. She tamped down the streak of panic those words generated. She could do many things, but the men she'd known had destroyed her faith in trust.

'Hold onto me, step in and sit down while I steady it with my foot. It won't sink, promise.' His lips curved into a reassuring smile that raced to his eyes as he coaxed her into the boat.

But it wasn't the boat trip that worried her. It was holding his hand. She could act all independent, avoid touching him and scramble into the boat on her own. She calculated that against the risk of upending the medical supplies into the salt water.

The medical supplies won. She reached out and caught his hand with her own, her fingers dwarfed in his wide palm. His heat fused with hers, racing through her, reigniting all the places that had glowed at his touch once before.

'Nothing like an adventure, right?' His solid, dependable tone encased her.

He was worried she was freaking out over the boat. If only it was that simple. 'I'm always up for an adventure.' She plastered a fake smile on her face and lowered herself into the round boat, ignoring the vague sense of loss that speared her when she let go of his hand.

Tom and the fisherman took their places in the basket boat, and the fisherman started to propel it forward using a single wooden paddle.

'We act as counterweights so lean back and enjoy the view.' Tom slid on sunglasses against the glare of the sun.

Sparkling turquoise water surrounded them as they headed toward an island dotted with coconut palms and golden sands. A conical mountain rose in the middle, dominating the landscape with its jungle green canopy. 'If this was in Far North Queensland, this place would be an exclusive tourist resort. I'm guessing it became a leper colony a long time ago.'

Tom nodded. 'The Catholic Church started this colony in the early 1900s, back in the days when the isolation of lepers from the general community was thought to be the way to stop the disease from spreading.'

'But the world knows now that leprosy is not transmitted by touch.'

His shoulders rose and fell in a resigned shrug. 'But in some local communities in Africa and Asia attitudes are slow to change. Lepers are still shunned. We're working on change and some will take place in our lifetime, but it's a long, slow process.'

She glanced up at the mountains that seemed almost to join the colony to the mainland. 'Is the only way to get here by boat?'

'Boat or a rugged jungle trek. Technically it's not an island but for all intents and purposes it may as well be. It's hard to walk when you're missing parts of your legs. The bigger boat left earlier with Hin, the supplies and the rice that Health For Life organized.'

As gentle waves washed the boat up onto the sand, children appeared from behind the trees, waving and running up and down the beach. Tom clambered out of the boat and started unloading the packs.

'We always get a big welcome when we visit. The kids really suffer from the isolation of the island. If one member of their family has leprosy then the whole family has to move to the village. As their parents are not welcomed in the towns they are stuck here until they're older. Even then they can experience prejudice when looking for work or trying to attend high school on the mainland.'

The fisherman handed Bec out of the boat and she and Tom walked up the beach, toward some low-roofed buildings.

Bec mulled over how such a beautiful natural setting had become a prison. 'So this false paradise is both a home and a hospital?'

'It's like any other village, except the two hundred people here can't leave to work. Those that can grow rice and fish but the poverty here is dire. When you're missing an arm or a leg, the physical work of farming is pretty much impossible.'

Tom grimaced. 'There isn't a hospital here. They have a medical clinic with health aides. If they need surgery they have to go to a provincial hospital. That creates its own set of problems. We don't run a clinic here but we provide bandages, gauze and dressing supplies, which are always needed.'

'What about crutches and artificial limbs?'

'We work with some charities to source those when we have patients who need them. Today we're going to do some skin checks and help the health workers.' He slowed his pace. 'Bec.'

The tone of his voice made her pause. 'Yes?'

'It can be pretty confronting if you've never seen the ravages of leprosy before.' Again his eyes shone with concern.

The feeling of being cared for welled inside her, warming her.

Scaring her.

'Thanks for the heads up.' With a monumental effort she dragged her eyes away from his, away from the feeling of wanting to fall into their softness and be cared for. But she cared for herself, that was how it had to be. *You're here to work.*

The clinic was L-shaped. Concrete walls were painted a bright cheery yellow and blue shutters lined the windows. The low thatched roof sloped downward and was rimmed by wide gutters to cope with the monsoon rains. Bec gave a wave to Hin, their interpreter. He stood chatting to people in an attractive courtyard dotted with flowering plants, and swept to within an inch of its life. Patients waited for their turn to see the health worker.

The peace and tranquillity of the tropical paradise setting clashed dramatically with the physical disfigurement of leprosy. Some people sat in wheelchairs— empty spaces below them where their legs should have been. Others had both legs but muscle contractures had left them bent and disfigured. One man was missing a hand, another an earlobe. Scarred eyes peered out of ulcerated faces, the cloudy whiteness of the pupils obscuring all vision.

Yet their calm smiles radiated a spirit of survival.

An elderly woman greeted her warmly, her gnarled, two-fingered hand gripping Bec's five-fingered one. *'Xin chào.'*

Bec repeated the oft-said greeting, which came out

sounding like *Sin jòw*. She knew immediately the task she would be working on for the day, and why a pallet of bandages had been delivered to the island.

She quickly got to work, setting up dressing packs.

'Even with the Multi-Drug Therapy, leprosy can never be totally removed from the body. But the damage can be limited to pale-coloured skin patches.' Tom spoke quietly while they worked together, debriding wounds. 'Many of the villages didn't have access to the antibiotic therapy that is offered today so by the time they got help, the bacterium that causes the lesions had led to a lot of skin thickening and nerve damage.'

'So they get peripheral neuropathy, which adds to the problems, right?' Bec's mind clawed back to find any memories of leprosy from nursing lectures. 'When part of the body is numb, the patient can't feel properly, which puts them at risk of injury and ulceration.'

She carefully snipped away the blackened skin around the edges of the wound on the old woman's leg, biting her lip in concentration.

Her patient gave her a toothy smile and patted her hand as if to say Don't worry, it doesn't hurt, keep going.

Tom's large hands belied the way his fingers could delicately debride a wound and carefully bind it with bandages. 'The extremities of the fingers and feet are hardest hit but the eyes can be involved and blindness is common.'

Tom spoke in Vietnamese to his patient as he taped the bandage in place.

The woman put her hands over his as her words floated out into the hot, humid air.

Tom smiled at her, shaking his head, his cheeks unusually bright for a man who seemed to take the heat in his stride.

Hin added a few words and then laughed a big belly-shaking laugh. Turning to Bec, he wiped his eyes. 'She says he has the touch of an angel but he should also use his hands to get himself a wife.'

The old woman nodded her head vigorously toward Bec.

Hin continued, 'She says you would be wise to choose a man with hands of delight.'

Bec forced out a polite laugh against a tight chest. It didn't seem to matter which side of the world she was on, patients always wanted to matchmake. It seemed to be an international hobby.

She caught Tom's gaze, wanting to share the ridiculous joke with him. His eyes, the colour of dark chocolate, held laughter and mirth, which confirmed that the old woman's idea was a preposterous notion.

His gaze flickered, a small flare of…what? She couldn't pin it down. Amusement quickly rolled in as his trade-mark grin streaked across his face at the ridiculous idea.

She laughed again, this time a true laugh, sharing the joke with someone who truly understood.

A sudden feeling of emptiness thudded through her. Crossly, she shrugged it away. People might want to matchmake but love didn't work for her. If she'd ever believed it could, she'd had the idea knocked out of her at twenty, proving how wrong she could be.

'What about the children, Tom? Do you skin-check

them when you visit?' She asked the question, needing to fill the silence between them.

'If their families are concerned, I check them out for lesions but all of them have had the preventative immunisation using the BCG vaccine.'

She wrinkled her nose. 'BCG—I thought that was for tuberculosis?'

He nodded. 'It is but it has a small protective effect against leprosy. As long as people don't come into repeated direct contact with the lesions, they're unlikely to get the disease.'

They worked consistently through to the end of the day. Bec lost count of how many different wounds she bandaged but she had a long list of items the villagers needed filed in her head. A Rotary Club at home might 'adopt' the village and source used crutches and wheelchairs. She'd write a few letters as soon as she had a chance.

'The village wants to give us a fish barbeque dinner at the beach.' Tom stowed away the last of the supplies. 'I'll race you there.'

She plonked her hat on her head. 'You're on!' She shot out the door ahead of him, racing along the neatly maintained gravel paths, dodging overhanging palm fronds and brilliant purple bougainvillea.

As her foot hit the sand, Tom dashed past her, straight into the middle of a children's soccer game. He ran backwards, dribbling their ball, his face alive with the joy of life. 'Come on, join in.'

As she watched him, a companionable and easy warmth spiralled inside her, relaxing her. *This* was exactly the sort of uncomplicated situation with Tom that she could handle.

She paused to catch her breath then jogged over to one end, taking her place next to the diminutive goalie.

'Stop ball,' instructed the boy, who looked about ten.

A line in the sand marked the goal. Bec smiled at his determined expression and nodded. 'Stop ball.'

With yells and squeals the children charged up and down the beach, dribbling, kicking and bouncing the ball off their heads. Bec was struck by the similarities between Australian and Vietnamese kids—they all loved soccer.

Tom enjoyed keeping possession of the ball and his height gave him a great advantage. Undeterred, the children's legs powered through the sand, their arms pulling at his shirt, trying to take him down.

She tried to imagine what he would have looked like as a kid playing sport, although he would have played Aussie backyard cricket.

He turned to find her, his eyes seeking hers.

Almond-shaped eyes.

Eyes the identical shape of the kids' he was playing against.

Realisation thudded into place. She consciously had to breathe. Some Vietnamese blood ran in his veins. Somewhere in Tom's past he had a Vietnamese relation. How had she missed it before?

She'd spent three weeks with the man. *You've been too busy admiring his other assets.*

She shushed the voice in her head. Anyone could have missed the connection. His height, his Western nose and quintessential Australian manner gave scant clues. So why had he not mentioned it to her?

The game swirled around them but the ball didn't come near Bec or her buddy as most of the action was down the other end of the makeshift field.

The young goalie shuffled his feet in the sand.

Bec understood. Not only was being goalie a big responsibility, it was often downright boring.

Suddenly the ball hurtled towards them, high in the sky.

The young boy jumped valiantly and missed.

Bec threw herself sideways, arms outstretched. The skin on her palms burned as the ball hurtled into her hands. She rolled on the sand, clutching the precious trophy.

Cheers surrounded her. Small hands touched her back as she sat up. This was what she believed in. Children having a childhood, being able to play even when other things in their life were tough.

Larger hands hauled her to her feet as smaller hands continued to pat her. Golden arms hooked around her waist and suddenly she was airborne.

'Now, that's what I call a spectacular save.'

She looked down into dancing eyes, alive with exhilaration and the wonder of life. Happiness rushed through her. 'It was pretty special, wasn't it?'

He laughed as he set her feet back on the ground, his arm still holding her body against his. 'We can't have you getting too puffed up about it. I'll get the next one past you.' He ducked his head, his lips sweeping across hers with a feather-light touch. Almost imperceptible.

Battering every protective defence.

Desire thudded through her, sucking the breath from her lungs, stripping the strength from her legs.

And then he was running back down the beach.

Bec stood immobilised, her body tingling from head to toe, catapulted into sensory overload from the lightest touch she'd ever known. Her tongue darted out, tracing her lips. Tasting him. Tasting Tom.

Heat mingled with salt and spice and she savoured it, needing to memorise his scent and flavour. Keeping it with her, making it part of her.

She'd never been kissed like that before.

Kisses had always been demanding or threatening—taking, never giving. This had been neither of those things. This had been... *Wonderful. Amazing. Terrifying*.

She didn't want to feel like this.

She refused to feel like this. Feelings like this meant danger. She knew that. It was why she didn't get involved with anyone.

That was hardly a kiss, Bec. It was a dare.

She glanced over a sea of black-haired boys to the tall black-haired man, whose face was streaked with wiliness and who was aiming a ball straight at her.

It had just been a dare. Of course it had. Everything was the same as it had ever been between them. Colleagues who respected each other and got along well.

Then he grinned at her.

Part of her protective wall melted.

The ball shot straight past her, into the goal.

CHAPTER FIVE

'WHAT'S ON THE agenda today, boss?'

Tom looked up from reading the letter from his mother that Health For Life had couriered to him from Hanoi.

Bec sat down opposite him and bit into a croissant, the buttery flakes clinging to the edge of her lips.

He clenched his fist under the table to silence his fingers, that screamed to be allowed to brush the crumbs away. His lips tingled, demanding to kiss the crumbs away.

That was *not* going to happen.

He'd stolen a kiss at the soccer game two days ago. The memory of the softness of her lips against his had stayed with him, revisiting at regular intervals. He hadn't planned to kiss her, but when she'd looked at him with her eyes shining like sun-kissed water, with her warm body pressed in against his own and her hidden curves fitting against his body, a kiss had seemed like the most natural thing in the world.

But that didn't mean it had been the right thing to do or that he should repeat it.

He refilled his coffee cup with the strong, fragrant brew the Vietnamese specialised in. An early-morning heart starter. 'You can have a day off today and visit China Beach. It's Vietnam's premier surf beach. It's gorgeous and it was made really famous by a TV show.' His chatty tone sounded forced even to his own ears.

She narrowed her gaze, her face sceptical. 'Hmm, and are you taking the day off?'

He squirmed under her penetrating gaze. 'I have some paperwork to do.'

She sipped her coffee. 'Hin mentioned something about going to an orphanage.'

Hell. He'd wanted to go to this orphanage on his own. It was one of four left on his list to visit. He needed to study the records, the lists of children who had been housed there. He was looking for clues, a needle in a haystack. Hoping for some tiny piece of information that might send him to his biological mother and end his two-year search. '*I'm* visiting the orphanage.'

She set her cup down very carefully. 'Is that code for "You can't come, Bec?"'

Guilt twisted inside him. 'Anyone can visit an orphanage and, heaven knows, there are plenty of them.'

A flash of irritation rippled across her vibrant eyes, chased away by curiosity. 'But you would prefer to go on your own?'

Damn it. She was too perceptive. Nothing got past her. He'd have to bluff his way through this.

Act casual. 'I thought you'd enjoy a day off and you can take in some history at the same time.' *Liar.* 'But, sure, you're welcome to come. I do have some admin work to do there, but while I'm busy with that I'm sure the kids would love a visit from you. But personally I'd choose the day at the beach.'

She tilted her head and wrinkled her nose, considering his answer. 'Great. I'll just put on some sunscreen.' She stood up.

He breathed a sigh of relief. For the first time since they'd met she was actually showing some sense and taking time off.

She fixed him with a steely look. 'I'll be ready to leave for the orphanage in five minutes.' She walked out of the room.

Hell, she'd outplayed him again.

Nothing.

Tom pushed the slim folder away from him, trying to halt the familiar rush of sadness that threatened to overcome him.

Hopes raised. Hopes dashed.

Hin squeezed his shoulder. 'Records were destroyed in 1975. Sorry.'

Tom took in a deep breath at the familiar story. 'Yeah, thanks for trying.'

He thanked the orphanage administrator by presenting her with a gift, and then he left the office.

'You have three more orphanages left on your list?' Hin walked beside him.

'I have. But right now I think I need a break from this.'

Hin nodded, understanding on his face. 'Just let me know when, and I will come with you.'

'Thanks, mate. I appreciate your support.' Tom shook his interpreter's hand.

'Catch you later. Now I'm going surfing. You'll find Bec with the babies.' Hin grinned cheekily as he strolled out of the grounds.

Ever since the old woman had insisted that Bec was the woman for Tom, Hin had taken every opportunity to tease him about her.

Shaking his head at the need for humans to match-make, he crossed the yard toward the baby room of the orphanage. On the way he promised a group of primary school age boys a game of soccer after their classes had finished.

He pushed open the nursery door to a sea of cots. His heart contracted in pain. Sixty cots lined up in rows with only enough space between them for the staff to walk sideways up the narrow aisles. Babies lay on their backs, staring at mobiles, their little legs kicking out from blue and white gingham nappies.

Bec stood in the middle of the room holding a baby against her chest, her cheek resting against the crown of the child's head.

She raised her head and turned toward him, a trail of tears staining her face.

His heart lurched from one pain to another. Orphanages confronted every belief and value a person held, and offered up a brutal mix of reality and hope.

He flattened the urge to wrap her in his arms and protect her. Not that he could.

He made his way over to her, trying not to knock the cots. As he drew closer he realised the child she held was over a year old and his legs hung down against Bec, completely lacking in tone. His almond-shaped eyes, dark and blank, tore at him.

He plastered a smile on his face. 'Who have we here?'

'This is Minh. He's got mild cerebral palsy and I think his hearing is impaired.' Bec's voice cracked. 'I just had to pick him up. He looked so much like he needed a cuddle.'

'Every kid here needs a cuddle.' He ran his hand over the child's head. 'The staff do their best and we have some fabulous volunteers. They come for three months and run some great programmes in orphanages across the country.'

'But this little guy needs physiotherapy and probably a hearing aid.' Bec kissed the top of his head before laying him down in the cot, carefully placing a stuffed toy in his hands. 'In Australia his disability would be categorised as mild to moderate and there would be so much assistance he could get to maximise his potential.' She turned to him. 'He needs a loving home. What about overseas adoption? That would be perfect for this little guy.'

'No.' The word cut through the air, cracking harshly like a stock whip.

Bec started and flattened herself against the cot.

Hell. Regret showered through him. 'Sorry, I didn't mean to startle you.' He extended his hands palms upward, a gesture of appeasement. 'It's just that every Westerner thinks overseas adoption is the solution.'

'And you don't agree.' Her shoulders dropped, relaxing into their normal position. Her face studied him, keen with interest.

He shook his head. 'No, I don't. I think we improve things here so they can live in their country of origin.' His chest tightened. He walked toward the door, suddenly needing to get out of the crowded room, needing to be in the open space of the garden.

'And what if that isn't in their best interest?' Bec spoke the moment they were outside.

A muscle near his eye started to twitch. 'How can leaving their country be in their best interest?'

'Is institutionalised care in their best interest?' Her voice tugged at him.

He folded his arms across his chest. 'If they can be protected, well fed and schooled, yes.'

'But not loved?' Her words gently probed.

'The staff here care greatly.' Defiance clung to his words.

'I don't doubt that. But if their parents cannot care for them or have rejected them because of a disability, and no one else wants to welcome them into their family, surely that is a reason for overseas adoption?'

'Overseas adoption is not nirvana for any child. It creates a unique set of problems. Problems that can be greater than the ones they face here.'

'I find that hard to believe.' She raised her chin, her jaw jutting out in a streak of stubbornness.

'You have no idea what you're talking about.' Frustration screamed inside his chest, desperate for release.

Her brows shot to her hairline. 'Oh, right, and you do? You've gone all political on me.' Indignation laced her words. 'There's a little boy in there with vacant eyes because he has no stimulation. He's cut off from participating in the world because he can't hear. With no access to physio and splints he'll have no opportunity to walk, either. But you're telling me he's better off here, deaf and crippled? Oh, please, give me a break.'

Exasperation spilled over. 'He'll know who he is and how he fits into the world. *His* life won't be filled with unanswered questions.' Blood pounded in his ears. He needed to stop this conversation. 'It's hot. I'll shout you a sugar-cane juice.'

He started to walk toward the street vendor outside the orphanage gates. *'Mia da.'* He held up two fingers and handed over the money.

The vendor pushed sugar-cane stalks through a large mangle, the contents dripping down into a plastic jug. He added lime juice as he poured the sticky liquid into two glasses.

Bec had already seated herself on a low plastic chair under a large, shady tree. Tom put the glass down in front of her on a small table and sat down.

'Thanks.' She picked up the glass, sipping the refreshing drink.

Silence hung between them. They sat watching the usual bustle of cyclos and motorbikes weaving around the pedestrians. Street vendors carried rambutans and dragon fruit in baskets, which hung from long bamboo poles that rested on their shoulders.

Tom relaxed, letting the noise of the street drive away the disappointment of the day. Soaking up the place of his birth even though he was no closer to finding any answers about his mother.

Bec drained her glass and put it down on the plastic cloth. She glanced up at him, her face neutral, with no sign of her previous indignation. The lines around her eyes crinkled slightly as she spoke. 'You're an overseas adoptee, aren't you?'

Her words barrelled into him with the force of a cannon, leaving a trail of emotional destruction in their wake. He'd dodged every question she'd ever asked him about his personal life. He hated the curiosity factor his story generated. But this time her question had hit with pinpoint accuracy and he had no place to hide.

Bec watched the colour drain from his face, emphasising his high cheekbones and the hint of black stubble around his mouth. Handsome and hurting.

She forced herself to stay silent and waited for him to speak.

He took in a deep breath. 'I was born in Vietnam but I was part of Operation Babylift and was evacuated for overseas adoption at the end of the war.'

Surprise rocked her. 'Oh, my God, you're part of this country's history, part of Australia's history.' She'd read all about the mass evacuation of children as Saigon fell.

He nodded, his brow creasing in amazement that she knew the story. 'Thousands of orphans were bundled onto planes and taken out of the country. Most went to the US but about two hundred and fifty of us went to Australia.'

He sounded like he was reciting from a textbook.

Factual, completely unemotional.

Protecting himself. A shaft of pain gripped her heart. 'How old were you?' Her voice sounded unusually soft.

'One month. I had a note pinned to me with my date of birth on it. I was pretty sick, malnourished and de-hydrated. Mum—my adopted mother—says I was the scrawniest baby she'd ever seen.' He smiled, his face alight with a memory.

She looked at the tall, healthy man across the table from her, marvelling at how he'd overcome such a tough start in life. 'You've certainly made up for it. Must have been all that fresh country air in Victoria.'

'That's me. I'm a walking advertisement for Dad's dairy products.' He grinned at her, white teeth flashing against a tanned face.

A deep, familiar longing spread through her at his smile. She set it aside, concentrating on Tom. 'Do you know anything about your biological parents?'

He shook his head. 'The note said, "Father dead. I love you."' His voice cracked. 'There was no name, and the note wasn't signed.'

She reached out without thinking, stroking his arm, needing to support him. Feeling his pain. 'Do you think your dad was a foreign serviceman?'

He gave a wry grin. 'With this nose, I think that's a given. He could have been Australian, American, perhaps French. Who knows? But my birth mother was Vietnamese.'

'You've got her expressive eyes.' The words had slipped out before she knew it.

He picked up her hands, encasing them in his larger ones. 'Thank you, that's the loveliest thing you could have said. I would dearly love to know what she looked like.' His hands stayed resting over hers.

Warm.

Soothing.

Connecting.

His heat travelled through her on a river of bliss. She struggled to think. 'So you came to Vietnam to find your mother?'

'I came to Vietnam to find me.'

His stark words tore at her heart. The adopted child with a vacant family tree.

His breath shuddered out on a sigh. 'I grew up in rural Victoria, the only Eurasian kid within a hundred kilometres. Before I was thirteen I didn't think much about how I had come to be with my family. I just got on with growing up. I was an Aussie just like my mates. I belonged to the footy club, the cricket club and I helped Dad with the milking.

'There was the occasional comment about my eyes from the school bullies but I had good friends and most of that washed over me. Although I guess I did wonder why I was being singled out. I didn't feel different but the kids had noticed.'

'And then the hormones kicked in?' She knew all about that. She vividly remembered starting to question everything about her own family.

The color of his brown eyes deepened as a shared understanding crept in. 'That's right. Suddenly I had so many more questions than I had answers. "Who am I? Why did she give me up?" I didn't feel I belonged in Australia and I didn't know anything about Vietnam, I couldn't even speak the language.'

'Halfway between East and West?'

'Something like that.' His fingers trailed across the backs of her hands, tracing each finger.

Mini-explosions of bone-melting desire whipped through her, zapping her concentration. She delved deep, needing to keep on track, needing to hear his story.

'Mum's a nurse and one day when I was being a right pain at sixteen she suggested I go back to Vietnam as an adult, and give something back to the country that had tried so hard to keep me but couldn't.'

'She's a really wise woman.' Bec pushed away the sadness about her own mother who hadn't been able to find the wisdom or the help to save herself. To save her daughter. 'So you're here and you're giving back. Is it helping?'

He dropped her hands and sat back, avoiding her gaze. 'This is my country. *My* people.' His voice emphasised the words but frustration crossed his face.

'What about your Australian mum and dad? How do they feel now?'

'They've only ever encouraged me. At the start they joined me in the search, but their life is in Australia.' A muscle spasmed in his jaw, his shoulders stiff and defensive. 'And my life is here. Vietnam is the missing bit of me.'

A niggling feeling pricked her. His body said one thing and his words another. Did the truth fall between?

'You're still searching for your mother?'

He nodded. 'This orphanage visit is part of that diminishing search. We've no idea which orphanage I came from.' He shrugged. 'I do it in stages. You need to gear up for this sort of thing.'

A stream of white-shirted children with red ties and blue shorts filled the orphanage grounds, their excited voices competing with the noise of the traffic. School was out.

Tom stood up quickly, the small plastic chair toppling behind him. 'I promised the boys a game of soccer. I'll catch up with you later.'

He'd deliberately ended the conversation as if he regretted telling her his story. She watched him walk away from her and stride toward the boys. Stride toward what he knew, aligning himself with people who understood. Kids abandoned like himself.

She had this utterly ridiculous feeling of wanting to hold him tight and shield him from the world. Make everything better for him. Find his mother.

But no one's life was perfect and no one's parents, real or imaginary, ever lived up to expectations.

Perhaps one day she should tell him that.

Sighing, she headed back to the nursery, planning to give Minh another cuddle. Hoping to see a spark of interest in his eyes.

CHAPTER SIX

Bᴇᴄ ᴍᴀɴᴀɢᴇᴅ ᴛᴏ carefully remove an insect that had become lodged in a ten-year-old's ear. Heaven knew how long the bug had been in there but it was causing a festering infection and hearing loss.

Simple things could quickly become severe and disabling as medical attention wasn't readily available in remote villages. As she applied antibiotic drops, Hin translated the continuing treatment for the child's mother.

'I hope they follow the instructions.' She waved goodbye to the girl and her mother and then turned and smiled at Hin. 'Take a break. I think we both need it.'

She and Tom were doing physical examinations on the children in a poverty-stricken village in the central highlands, a couple of hours drive inland from the coast. Her mind continued to grapple with the fact that children here had to leave school after receiving the most basic education, to work and earn money for the family. This diminished their prospects to go on and really improve their lives and those of their families.

Sweat beaded into droplets and rolled down her

stomach. How she wished she could be in shorts and a vest top with a breeze against her skin. But it wasn't an option.

She glanced around and waved to Tom, who was walking toward her, holding some cool drinks in one hand and balancing some sweet sticky rice pyramids in the other, the distinctive banana leaf wrapping green against his palm.

He always brought her over a snack and insisted she take a break. He did it in his quiet, laid-back, no-fuss way. She often wondered if this was an innate part of him or something he'd learned from practical farming parents. Country hospitality personified.

A blend of unease and longing shimmered through her. She could get used to this sort of caring. She treasured it each and every time it happened.

And she hated it that she did. *Depending on someone makes you weak.* She would never again open herself up to being that vulnerable.

Tom smiled as he handed over the afternoon snacks. 'You've been spraying your clothes with permethrin, right?'

She rolled her eyes. 'Yes, Tom. And I have been sleeping under my permethrin-impregnated mosquito net.' That wasn't strictly true but she wasn't about to tell him the real story.

Each night she lay underneath the mosquito net attempting sleep. But whenever she closed her eyes, images of Tom would waft through her mind—Tom playing soccer, his athletic frame nimbly kicking the ball, Tom racing her to the beach, his long stride easily carving up the distance, Tom's hands gently encircling her waist, his body's length against her own, and his lips grazing hers with the most tender touch she'd ever known.

She shook away the image, swinging her hair off the back of her neck. 'I've also stopped using my perfume and discarded my show-no-dirt navy for this pale green colour.' She grimaced at the streaks of dirt already evident.

'Want to go home, city girl?' He grinned again, his banter dancing around her.

She laughed. 'No, but one night soaking in a tub filled with bubbles would be utter bliss.'

His twinkling eyes darkened for a moment before a spark of desire flared in their depths.

A wave of heat exploded deep down inside her, streaking through her like a rocket-fuelled missile. What had she *not* been thinking? What had possessed her to talk about bubble baths with him? She'd learned years ago to dress non-sexually and not to draw attention to herself as a woman.

That way she couldn't be hurt. But here she was, hurling an image of herself naked out between them, breaking every rule.

He cleared his throat. 'How many children do you have left to see?' His husky words hung between them.

'I don't know. Enough.' She busied herself with her equipment, not risking looking at him, scared she might again see desire in his eyes.

Scared because she wanted to see desire again in his eyes.

Just plain scared.

He stood silently, deep in thought. Watching her.

Finally, he shoved his hands in his pockets and turned to go. 'Right, well, I'll leave you to get on with it.'

His thoughtfulness prickled against her fear like a burr caught in a sock. 'Thanks for the rice and the water but, really, you didn't need to bother.' The moment the words had left her mouth she wanted to snatch them back. She'd just taken away her thanks and turned them into a criticism.

He shrugged and spoke quietly. 'I realise you've had to look after yourself for a long time, Bec, and that's made you very independent. But part of being on a team is looking out for other team members. You might think about letting someone take a moment to do that for you every now and then.'

He walked away, his shoulders stiff.

Guilt poured through her. In her struggle to stay immune from this gorgeous man she'd just stomped on his feelings and hurt a person who'd always treated her with respect.

Tom wanted to chop wood. Wanted to swing the axe high over his head and bring it slamming down into the timber, sending splinters flying. He needed to feel the release of tension, feel it drain out of him and into the axe.

He'd lived at the woodpile during his adolescence. There was nothing more satisfying than splitting wood when that hot ball of fury sat firmly in your chest.

But he had patients to see.

He clenched and unclenched his hands. Bec Monahan was the most provoking, the most maddening, most independent, most... His brain fumed, clutching for more descriptors.

Most sexy woman you have ever met.

Visions of her in a bubble bath resurfaced in his mind. He blasted it away on a wave of outrage. What the hell was he thinking, picturing Bec naked?

She was gorgeous but she deserved someone who could give her his complete attention. Right now he couldn't do that. He had to sort out who he was before he could get involved with any woman.

Not that she wanted him anyway.

Since she'd told him about her father she'd seemed more relaxed around him. The flinching thing had faded, thank goodness. He hated feeling like an ogre just because he was male. And yet she still had this wall around her, keeping more out than she let in.

This woman gave of herself every moment of her day but if he tried to give some of that care back to her, she refused it every time.

What the hell was wrong with her? Couldn't a bloke be a friend?

Her father threw her down the stairs.

He closed his eyes and drew in a long, slow, deep breath. He had no idea what it was like to live in fear but Bec had lived with it for sixteen years. Ironically, he'd fled a war as a baby and she had lived through a domestic war.

But she'd moved on from that and had made herself a fulfilling life.

A life on her own.

Alone.

His anger died. She'd been so busy surviving she hadn't learned the wonder of friendship.

Teach her how to let people in. Show her friendship.

The crazy thought ricocheted through his head. Could he?

'Tom! Hin! Code one.' Bec's voice carried across the compound from where she stood by the door of a house waving frantically.

Since the cholera outbreak they had instigated a series of codes to signal each other. Code one meant medical emergency. He grabbed the emergency kit from the four-wheel-drive and ran back to her.

A toddler, about eighteen months old, lay in an oval bamboo basket in the dark hut. Her mother knelt next to her, her face taut with fear.

Bec rubbed the tiny girl's sternum. 'I can't rouse her. She's unconscious. No head injury evident and her skin is burning up.' Her worried face glanced up at him. 'And I can't find Hin.'

Tom recognised the mother. He'd seen this child a couple of months earlier. In Vietnamese he asked the woman, 'Did she take all the medicine in the bottle?' He hoped his accent was on the correct vowels of the Vietnamese words.

The mother wrung her hands and dropped her eyes.

Tom caught sight of the family temple with the bottle of Artemisinin placed firmly in the centre, flanked by other offerings of flowers, food and incense.

Exasperation slammed into hurt. Why didn't they listen to his advice? He wasn't just some foreigner charging in. He was Vietnamese, too. He was on their side.

Just treat the child. He gently inserted the aural thermometer into the little girl's ear. 'Bec, she's got a temp of forty-two Celsius. Set up a drip.'

Bec nodded. 'Saline?'

'No, glucose. It's malaria and she's going to need sugar. Severe malaria causes a precipitous fall in blood sugar, inducing a coma.'

He gently opened the eyelids of his patient, shining a penlight into her eyes. 'Cerebral malaria can mimic a head injury or meningitis, but I diagnosed malaria on this child a while ago with a finger-prick test.'

'It's hard to treat it when the malaria in South-East Asia is extremely resistant to drugs.' Bec threw him an understanding look.

'I prescribed ACT. It works well, it just has to be taken.' He inclined his head as his anger blasted out the words.

Bec caught site of the bottle, frowning as comprehension dawned.

Hin rushed in. 'What's happening?'

Bec spoke first. 'Cerebral malaria. Can you go and get the ice? I need to cool her down fast. Bring towels as well.'

Hin nodded and turned, running out of the hut.

Tom put his finger on the sole of the child's foot, pushing his nail into the skin to try and rouse her to the stimulus. 'Hell, that's a zero on the Blantyre coma scale.'

'No response to painful stimulus and she's not even crying. She's critical.' Bec pushed a torch into the mother's hand and moved the light beam onto the child's arm. 'Hold it here, please.'

The English words meant nothing to the mother but Bec's active demonstration said it all.

Bec swabbed the arm and handed Tom a tiny cannula. 'She needs to be in intensive care.'

Tom guided the needle into the flaccid arm, concentrating on not going right through the vein. 'We'll get her there but first let's get some fluid and antipyretics into her to bring the fever down.'

She bit her lip and taped the drip in place, putting a backboard on the tiny arm.

Tom's heart contracted. He wanted to tell Bec that the child would be all right but he couldn't provide that guarantee. All he had were facts and stats. 'Toddlers succumb to malaria because they've just been weaned. They lose their mother's antibodies before they can develop some resistance of their own.'

Bec stroked the child's head. 'Come on, little one, hang in there.' With a flick of her head she turned to him, the worry in her eyes replaced by her practical go-get-'em attitude. 'Obviously you won't have Mannitol in that emergency kit to reduce the swelling of the brain, so what's your next step? I know you have more up your sleeve than sugar and paracetamol.' Her encouraging smile carried total belief in his skills.

Her compliment rallied his dented spirit. He smiled at her, longing to tell her how much her faith in his ability as a doctor really helped. 'Quinine is still the drug of choice and we'll push that after we've brought her fever down. I don't want her fitting if I can help it.'

Hin rushed back into the hut, clutching the portable cooler and towels. Bec quickly rolled the ice into the towels to make small ice packs, which she placed around the little girl, wedging them between the child and the basket.

Tom titrated the paracetamol into the IV. 'Hin, explain to the mother that her daughter has malaria and she must go to Danang hospital.'

Hin's voice relayed the message.

A howl of distress sounded from the mother, her face taut with grief.

'She says Danang is too far and they have no money to pay the hospital.'

'Tell her I'll pay.' Bec wrapped her arms around the woman's shoulders, comforting and supporting her.

Hin looked straight at Tom, seeking clarification.

He nodded. 'Tell her the bills will be paid no matter what.' Money might not be enough to save the child. Sighing, he did another set of observations.

No change.

This little girl was in a deep coma. The malaria might have paralysed her, damaged her hearing and her sight. 'We need to get this little girl to Danang as soon as possible. Put the back seats down in the four-wheel-drive. It's just turned into an ambulance.'

'Does Danang have the facilities to cope with such a sick child?' Bec's wide-eyed, anxious face, stared at him.

'Yes, if we can get her there alive.' The words came out flat. He'd come to Vietnam to find himself, truly connect with his country of birth. But how the hell could he do that if they refused to accept him as one of them?

And how could he give back if they refused his treatment?

The ever-present seeds of displacement suddenly

sent up shoots of doubt. Strong, green and pervasive, they entwined around his heart and soul.

You don't belong anywhere.

He scooped the child into his arms, refusing to listen to the words that haunted him every day.

Tom meticulously laid pieces of driftwood on top of each other in the fire pit he'd dug in the sand.

'Did you belong to the Scouts?' Bec's laughing voice washed over him.

He looked up from his kneeling position to see her smiling down at him, the slight breeze whipping her soft hair around her face. Whipping the shapeless cotton trousers and jacket onto her body, outlining pert breasts and round hips. His blood stirred.

He cleared his throat. 'I was in the Scouts for awhile, but it was Dad who taught me how to make a fire.' He lit a match, watching the small yellow and blue flame curl around the paper and catch the kindling.

He'd spent the day at the hospital. Miraculously he'd managed to keep little Kim alive on the long, slow journey to Danang. He'd reluctantly handed her over to the care of the physicians at the hospital but had stayed around until she'd shown definite signs of improvement.

Bec had virtually pushed him out the door at five o'clock. On the way home she'd completely floored him when she'd asked him to show her China Beach. It was the first social thing she'd initiated since he'd met her. She usually disappeared into her room at the end of a working day mumbling excuses ranging from washing her hair through to writing letters to Rotary Clubs.

She'd even offered to shout him dinner at a hawker's stall. But on an impulse he didn't want to examine very closely, he'd found himself insisting that he'd cook dinner for her at the beach. They'd stopped at a market and bought fish, coriander, chilli, beer and rice. Everything he needed for a China Beach barbecue.

'Can I help with anything?' Bec hovered.

He noticed she didn't do 'just sitting' very well. 'No, I've got it sorted. We'll just let the fire burn down to embers and I'll cook the fish. Right now all we have to do is sit.' He grinned at her disconcerted look.

The sun, a blazing orange ball, slid silently closer to the mountains that curved around the coast, its last rays turning the South China Sea from blue to a fiery red. Spreading out the picnic rug, he sat down next to her, slightly closer than she normally sat next to him. He waited for her to move away.

A slight tremor raced across her shoulders but she smiled brightly and stayed put. 'I love sitting on a beach and seeing the sun set. I spent a lot of time on Cottesloe beach in Perth. It became a refuge for me.' Her matter-of-fact voice belied all she'd been through.

It took all of his self-control not to put his arm around her shoulder and hug her close. 'I reckon my mum must have come from the coast. I've always hankered to have the sting of salt in my nostrils. When I'm in the south I always make sure I come to the beach. I always feel at peace here.'

'I guess the farm was a long way from the coast.' She tucked her hair behind her ears as she looked at him.

'No, the farm's only a half-hour drive from the sea.

Dad used to take me fishing at Corner Inlet and I was never more content than when I was sitting in that tinnie boat with a fishing rod in my hand.' A wistful memory stirred inside him.

'Makes you think about nature versus nurture, doesn't it?' Her relaxed face glowed with the rays of the setting sun. 'You grew up close to the ocean and your adopted dad was a keen fisherman. We could hypothesise that your love of the sea comes from companionable times sitting in a boat with your dad.'

Resentment swirled in his gut as her comment snagged against his ideas about his biological mother. '*You* could hypothesise that.' He opened the food bag and pulled out two bottles of beer, jerking the seals off with more force than necessary.

People had no idea what it was like to know nothing about their family. 'You grew up with the mannerisms of your parents and grandparents, knowing who they came from. I bet someone in your extended family wrinkles their nose like you do.'

She accepted the proffered beer with a nod of thanks. 'Sure, but did I see my mother do that and copy her, or is it embedded in my DNA?'

'Twin studies would say it's in your DNA.' His words shot back hard, fast and uncompromising.

Surprise streaked across her face. 'No, twin studies would say that under certain environmental conditions genetic traits may come to the fore…or not. If you had lived inland then you wouldn't have had the opportunity to fall in love with the sea, and you probably wouldn't have missed it.'

She spoke softly, understanding on her face. 'I think you need to believe your mother came from this area so you can hang your hat on something, try and place yourself in a particular part of Vietnam, so you feel that you belong.'

Fear tore through him. How the hell had she worked that out? 'Yeah, well, belonging is just a fantasy. A little girl nearly died of malaria because I don't belong.'

Disbelief and confusion played across her face. 'What on earth do you mean?'

All his anguish of the day rushed back, installing itself inside his cavities of doubt. 'If I'd grown up here, Kim's mother would have listened to me, administered the ACT, and Kim would have recovered without developing cerebral oedema.' His fingers, taut with tension, gripped the beer bottle.

'I wouldn't bet on it.' Her eyes flashed. 'We're talking about people who have limited education. Ask Hin. I bet he wasn't surprised that they used the medication as an offering. Especially when they believe that all things good come from their favoured deity.'

He bristled at her words. 'But at least I would have understood that might happen and I could have done something to prevent it.'

'Really?' She raised her brows, her eyes full of questioning doubt. 'I don't think Hin has much understanding of how to stop it and he's university educated.'

'But I would have been a doctor fluent in the language, accepted by the community, someone to look up to. They would have listened to me.'

She held his gaze, seeing into his soul. 'If you'd

grown up here, you might not have even finished primary school, let alone become a doctor.'

Her quiet words slugged him, ripping into traitorous, questioning thoughts he'd hidden away deep inside himself. He didn't want to hear this, didn't want to revisit those thoughts. He stood up. 'I would *always* have been a doctor.'

Tom's words, laced with determination but mingling with pain, evaporated into the evening air. Bec swallowed a sigh. He truly believed he'd been ripped away from his country of birth and therefore was a lesser person in the eyes of the Vietnamese.

How could an intelligent man get it so very wrong? He did amazing work here. He needed to talk to local doctors and hear their frustrations about lack of patient compliance. Had he conveniently forgotten his Australian patients and their lack of compliance? She was sure the stories from home would match the Vietnamese stories. Lack of compliance crossed cultural borders.

He strode over to the fire and grabbed the shovel. With a side-to-side action he spread out the coals ready to accommodate the fish he'd wrapped in banana leaves. His shirt moved fluidly across his shoulders.

An image of her hands exploring taut, rippling muscles bombarded her, a pool of yearning welling up deep within her. She closed her eyes and breathed in deeply. This unwanted physical attraction was getting harder and harder to control.

Throwing her head back, she gazed up into the night sky at the bright pinpricks of the early rising stars. The beach was blissfully quiet, all the hawkers having retreated for their own evening meal. Bright blue and red fishing boats were heading out to sea for the night, their lights glittering in the reflections of their wakes.

She stood up and walked down to the water, leaving Tom to have the space he obviously wanted. She stepped into a small wave, welcoming the warm water as it rolled across her feet. It may be seven o'clock at night but when the difference between the maximum and minimum temperature was only five degrees Celsius, any time was hot. She stared out into the night and thought about all the things she'd experienced in such a short time. She thought of Minh, whom she'd visited again earlier in the day, and the joy she'd experienced when he'd smiled at her. She'd been doing some stimulation work with him and the other babies. How on earth was she was ever going to settle on *one* project idea?

'Dinner.' Tom's voice brought her back to the present and she jogged up the beach. They sat crossed-legged, eating the steamed fish and rice with their fingers.

She threw her banana leaf into the fire. 'That was absolutely sensational. The flavours of coriander and chilli go together so well.' She licked a few grains of rice from the corner of her mouth.

Tom's eyes followed the movement. 'All we need is the moon and it would be perfect.' His voice, deeper than usual vibrated around her as he lay back on the rug, resting on his elbows.

Glorious rivers of liquid heat wound through her. *Tom and moonlight.* The idea appealed and appalled simultaneously, making her dizzy.

She wriggled her toes in the sand. 'Thanks.'

'You're welcome. I love cooking a barbecue.'

Now would be a good time to apologise for being so snaky at the village.

She turned and lay on her side, facing him. 'No, I don't mean for dinner.' She could feel his heat caressing her skin, creating minitornadoes of sensation thudding through her. Muddling her thoughts. 'Well, yes, of course, I do mean thanks for dinner but not just dinner.'

Flustered, her words jumbled and tumbled over each other. 'I mean, thanks for everything. I foisted myself on you and over these last few weeks you've looked out for me. Like you said, it's what people do and I haven't been very good at being part of the team.'

She tugged at some burrs caught on the rug. 'I'm really sorry I snapped at you yesterday. I appreciate all you do. I guess I'm just not used to people taking the time to check up on me. So, thanks.'

He gave her arm a quick squeeze. 'It's no biggie.'

His brief touch made her ache for more. 'No, really it is. Most men I know are completely selfish.' The moment she'd spoken the words, regret heaved through her.

His smile morphed into a quizzical expression demanding more information 'Really? As a species, we're not all bad. Perhaps you need to get out more and meet the less selfish ones.'

'Nah, staying in is a lot easier.' She kept her tone light and sat up, facing back out to sea. 'Relationships only end in tears.'

'Someone break your heart, Bec?' She heard his soft words from behind her.

She thought of those dark few months in a tiny apartment in Perth when all her childhood dreams of a handsome prince changing her life had vaporised. 'He tried to break my heart and me. But I got wise and left with some bruises and my heart battered but not broken. Determined but intact.'

A shudder ran the length of his body and he was quiet for a moment. He cleared his throat. 'I've got contacts, you know, I could have him taken out. I've done it for other girls.' His humour wrapped her up in supporting comfort.

She laughed. 'You're just the sort of friend a girl needs.'

'I've got lots of friends who are women.' His voice suddenly became serious as he sat up next to her, imitating her position of knees drawn up to chin.

'Just friends, not girlfriends?'

He shrugged. 'Girlfriends are high maintenance. I don't have time for that right now. They want to settle down and I can't do that yet.'

'Ah, the typical Generation X male, the commitment-phobe.'

'Yeah, that's right.' A tick appeared in his jaw in complete contrast to his bantering tone.

She didn't believe his words.

He leaned in, his shoulders playfully bumping hers. 'I make a good friend, Bec. Trust me. Let me show you the joys of friendship and redeem the image of men.'

Trust me.

If only it were that easy.

His heat called to her. His arm touched her arm, his side flanked her side, his knees caressed her knees. Tingling sensations exploded the full length of her body.

He'd just admitted he didn't want anything from her or any woman except friendship.

He's offering friendship. Friendship is safe, right?

She pushed him back with her shoulders, gently nudging him. 'Friends, eh?'

He grinned, his eyes dancing in the firelight as he raised his palm to hers. 'It's a pact. Friends.'

'Friends.' She ignored the streak of heat that raced through her at his touch, challenging the word.

CHAPTER SEVEN

BEC STOOD DWARFED beneath the thirty-seven-metre flagpole, the distinctive red flag with the central yellow star fluttering high and proud above her. She turned one hundred and eighty degrees and stepped back in time.

Built high atop a gated wall, Yin and Yang ceramic roof tiles gave the building its distinctive Chinese-style roof line. Intricate ceramic dragons and phoenixes draped the pitch of the roof, protecting and bringing prosperity. A temple flag, with its distinctive square shape, flew from the middle balcony, surrounded by carved ironwood balustrades. Bec could imagine an emperor in golden robes, holding court.

They were on their way back to Hanoi and Tom had said, 'No way could you miss Hué.' *Way* being the pronunciation of Hué, he'd chuckled at his play on words. He seemed to be very content with his metaphoric tour guide hat on. 'The citadel was the home of the Nguyen dynasty, the last imperial family of Vietnam. The defending wall encloses ten kilometres and is two metres thick.'

He gave a wry smile. 'Over the centuries, dynasties got rolled quite often by other war-lord families.'

'My head's spinning with temples, pagodas, tombs, dates, people and names.' Bec fanned herself with her hat as the indefatigable heat sapped her concentration.

Tom laughed. 'That happens to everyone the first time they come here. There's so much history and fabulous architecture to see. Hué was the central pulse of Vietnam for a long time, full of political intrigue and coups, as well as being the religious and educational capital. It's a fascinating place but it can wear you down.'

She smiled wanly. 'I think I just went into temple overload.'

He grabbed her hand. 'Must be time for ice cream.'

Five minutes later they sat by the Perfume River, sharing the biggest banana split Bec had ever seen. 'This vanilla ice cream is to die for.'

'The French left a few great legacies in this country and my favourites are baguettes, gateaux and ice cream.' He languidly licked his spoon, his tongue savouring the last traces of the creamy confection.

Bec's breath stalled in her throat as an image of his tongue exploring her body exploded in her mind. *Oh, no, don't go there.* She'd thought the knowledge that neither of them wanted a relationship would have nailed the lid closed on these unexpected bursts of hormone-fuelled lust. Especially since they'd made their friendship pact.

She'd been stunned at how easy it was to be his friend. On the surface nothing had changed between them since she'd opened herself up to his friendship, and yet everything had changed.

She couldn't quite put her finger on it. Tom was still Tom—kind, considerate, laid-back and fun. His respect for her as a colleague remained the same, and they worked together as a team. *But it's a stronger team.*

Was that it? Had she relaxed around him? Had he relaxed around her?

There were subtle changes. Like him grabbing her hand to pull her toward the ice-cream stall, a squeeze of her shoulder when she'd dealt with a tough case. There was a camaraderie that had been absent before and it warmed her in a way she'd never known. A secure warmth. A companionable warmth.

Perhaps Tom was right. Perhaps she'd missed out by being too self-contained and independent. She leaned back, full of ice cream but energised by the break in the shade. 'So what's next on the tour schedule?'

Tom checked his watch. 'I want to stop in at the Buddhist nunnery and do a check up on one of the elderly nuns.'

'A Buddhist nunnery? I had no idea. I've heard of Buddhist monks but not nuns.'

'They don't wear saffron robes, often they're brown or grey. But they're the best vegetarian cooks I've ever come across and they'll want to feed you.'

She rubbed her stomach. 'Now you tell me. Why did you let me eat such a huge sundae?'

He grinned his bone-melting smile. 'That's why we shared.' He left some notes and coins on the table and ushered her out the door, back to the waiting four-wheel-drive.

The vehicle wound up into the hills behind Hué, the

lush greenery contrasting with the dusty road. 'What's that?' Bec pointed to a roadside stall. Shaky wooden racks supported the most amazing display of vivid coloured sticks she'd ever seen. Red, green, purple and yellow sticks were tied together at their bases and fanned out in the shape of an ice cream cone.

'It's incense for the temples and it's big business in this area. Cinnamon and sandalwood trees grow along the banks of the Perfume River and they harvest the scent from the wood shavings. Would you like to see it being made?' Enthusiasm for the idea danced across his face.

She clapped her hands in delight. 'I'd love to if we have time.'

Tom gave her an indulgent smile. 'Sure, we can spare ten minutes.' He asked the driver to stop and they stepped up to one of the tiny stalls. A woman sat under cover at a small table, holding about thirty thin bamboo sticks, which had been painted red along three quarters of their length. Her hands rapidly rolled the sticks across a pile of fine dust, while she used a trowel with her right hand to scoop more powder over them.

Bec watched, fascinated. 'How does the scent stick to the bamboo?'

Tom pointed to a large glob of rolled up gooey-looking stuff. 'That's glue.'

The woman looked up from under her *non la* and smiled, pushing some sticks into Bec's hands.

Confused, Bec accepted them.

Tom laughed at her expression. 'Do you want to have a go at making some incense?'

Always up for anything new, she nodded. 'Sure, why not?'

Gripping the sticks with her left hand, she tried to roll the glue on evenly before attempting to dust it in the cinnamon powder. Laughing, she held up a wonky-looking stick. 'I can't seem to co-ordinate my hands.'

'Just as well you're not a surgeon.' Tom's laugh rumbled around her. He moved in, standing behind her, putting his hands over hers. 'You spin with your left and you push the trowel with your right, like this.'

She tried to concentrate on the motion of the bamboo and how his hands were moving hers. But every skerrick of attention evaporated the moment his body curved against hers. His breath caressed her neck, tickling and enticing, his chest moved up and down against her back, massaging her as he breathed, and his thighs were against her buttocks, fitting snugly.

Longing blazed through her, followed by delicious tingles sparking at every part of her body he touched. She wanted to drop the bamboo and turn in his arms, lay her head on his shoulder and just savour being held.

But that wasn't on offer. Friendship didn't cover that.

'That's it. Try again.' Tom's voice sounded like it was coming from far away, down a long, long tunnel.

With superhuman effort she pulled her concentration back to the incense.

He stepped back, breaking contact.

Her body ached. Every muscle, every fibre, every cell cried out at the loss of his touch.

She rolled the bamboo. She tossed the powder with the trowel and triumphantly held up an evenly coated stick.

'Hey, you did it.' He raised his hand above his head and gave her a high five and a wide grin. 'We'll buy some incense for the nuns and we better get going.'

They paid for five bunches of incense, each colour a different scent, bowed their thanks and drove the short distance to the nunnery.

Bec stepped out of the vehicle beside a wobbly bamboo fence, which circled a thriving vegetable garden. Somehow it kept out ambling pigs and long-legged chickens. In the distance she could see the quintessential Vietnamese image—an emerald rice paddy with a lone worker up to her waist in green, a conical hat on her head. 'Why are there graves in the rice paddies?'

Tom slung his medical pack onto his shoulder and walked with her toward the whitewashed building. 'They like to bury their dead on their property, keep them close. Then at Tết, the Vietnamese New Year, they call the dead back to visit, so it's easier if they're close.'

'Just to visit?' Bec wrinkled her nose, thinking about live relatives that often outstayed their welcome.

'Very wisely, they send them back at the end of Tết.' He gave a wry grin, understanding crossing his face. 'The nuns here range from fourteen through to eighty. They usually have a few children living here as well and occasionally women who are seeking refuge. The temple is a popular place for couples to visit before they have a baby or if they want to conceive.'

He paused at a fork in the gravel path. 'You go to the temple with the incense and meet some of the nuns. They'll show you around while I do the check-up and make sure my stubborn nun has been taking her digoxin.'

'Sounds like a plan.' She stood for a moment, watching him walk away. She treasured the moments she could watch him unobserved. Admiring how his hair tangled with his collar, the sway of his hips and the way the cotton of his shorts moved across taut buttocks.

She closed her eyes for a moment, forging the memory into her brain. She spun back, the gravel crunching under her sandals, and made her way to the entrance of the temple.

Slipping her feet out of her shoes and hanging her hat on a stand, she swung her leg over the high step into the dark interior of the temple. She bowed to the nun and placed the incense in a basket.

A young couple stood at the altar. They pushed a burning stick of incense into a sand pot which was nestled between a bowl of fruit and a vase of flowers. The woman rested one hand on her lower back and the other on her swollen belly. Her husband stood next to her, his arm across her shoulder, his gaze fixed on her face and a smile of adoration clinging to his lips.

Bec smiled. They would be making the offering for their unborn child and their future as a family—their dreams and hopes so clearly evident in their eyes.

Suddenly an empty feeling opened up inside her, spreading an icy chill through her like cold fingers reaching deep into places she thought she'd sealed off.

She tried to shrug off the feeling. What was wrong with her? 'Happy families' wasn't something she connected with herself. Relationships and her made a toxic combination. She'd never experienced anything good in a relationship.

What about Tom?

She pushed the thought out of her mind. Tom was a friend. Friendship was completely different.

She quickly stepped back into the daylight, leaving the temple and the couple behind her, and followed the neatly raked path toward the main house.

She rounded the corner and found another couple. Except this time the heavily pregnant woman was leaning over a bench, moaning.

A blond-haired man clutched the woman's arm. 'Sweetheart, you have to walk to the car.'

The unexpected English words sounded completely out of place in the garden. Bec ran over. 'Can I help? I'm a midwife.'

The Asian woman's hand curved around Bec's wrist, gripping hard and her large almond-shaped eyes implored her to help. 'Can't…get…to…hospital.' Her words shook with fright.

Confusion swamped Bec. The woman looked Vietnamese but sounded Australian. She glanced between husband and wife.

The man caught Bec's gaze. 'Oh, thank goodness, you're Australian!' The husband's voice trembled. 'She insisted on coming to this temple, even though I didn't want her to. It's our third baby and now…'

The woman moaned again, her fingernails cutting into Bec's arm.

'I'm Bec Monahan and I think we need to get your wife onto a bed so I can examine her.'

'I'm Mark and my wife is Melissa, and the baby isn't due for another three weeks.' His voice rose with worry. 'I'm working for Glaston International and we're living in Ho Chi Minh City. We've arranged for the delivery to be in the French hospital there, not up here in the middle of nowhere.' He spoke like a CEO. A man used to being in charge, having his orders obeyed and sticking to a plan. He seemed completely bewildered by the deviation.

Two young nuns ran up on hearing the noise and showed the way to a room. Mark swung Melissa into his arms and carried her there, gently lowering her onto the bed.

Bec spoke to the nuns. '*Bác sĭ*. Doctor.' She raised her hands to indicate a tall man. '*Bác sĭ.*'

They nodded and ran off to find Tom. Bec hauled out a pair of gloves from her bag. When she'd packed them she'd been thinking they'd be used for doing first aid or the washing-up, not delivering a baby. 'Melissa, I just want to see how far away you are from having this baby.'

She sucked in her lips and sent up a quick prayer that Melissa was just scared and overreacting to some early contractions. But the fact that this was her third pregnancy, combined with a lot of groaning, had Bec worried.

'At least in this heat my hands are warm,' Bec quipped, trying to lighten the tension. Using her hands, she examined the lie of the baby by palpating Melissa's abdomen. Limbs seemed to be everywhere. She pressed down on top of the uterus, feeling for the baby's bottom. It felt unusually hard.

She felt again, her fingers transmitting the unwanted information. 'Melissa, has your doctor mentioned anything about the baby's position?'

The woman shook her head and grunted.

Grunting wasn't good. 'I'm going to do an internal examination now.' Bec gently inserted two fingers, feeling for the cervix, but she could only detect a lip and bulging forewaters. She couldn't feel past the bulge to the presenting part. *Damn.* A fully dilated cervix ruled out getting back to Hué hospital to have the baby.

Not to worry. Babies basically delivered themselves. Melissa and Mark would have a surprise to take home to the family from their outing to the temple.

Melissa grunted as a strong contraction gripped her. Liquid gushed from her vagina.

Bec immediately removed her hand. A black substance stuck to the end of her gloved fingers. *Meconium.*

Bec's heart beat faster. 'I'm sorry, Melissa, I just have to go back one more time to feel the baby's position.' Her brain already knew but she needed to feel the presenting part to kick her disbelief out the door.

As her fingers reached she prayed to feel the hard, bony skull of the baby. Her fingers made contact. *Soft.*

Bec took in a deep breath and felt again. Soft and yielding.

No. She sent up a prayer of help to whoever was out there and listening. They were facing an obstetric emergency and about to deliver a breech baby with no equipment.

'What's happening?' Tom's cheerful voice reverberated around the room.

Bec glanced around over her shoulder. 'We're about to deliver a breech. Ask the nuns to boil water and bring towels.'

Tom stood perfectly still for a moment, his eyes glued to her face. His expression reflected all her emotions—fear, professionalism and relief they could back each other up.

'Breech! But isn't that bottom first?' Mark's anxiety morphed into terror.

Tom put his hand on the other man's shoulders. 'It is. But in an unlucky situation you have the fortune to have a midwife and a doctor here today. I'm Tom and I'm a doctor. You go and hold your wife's hand and leave the rest to Bec and me.'

Bec was certain his words indicated more control than either of them felt.

Tom hauled open his medical kit, passed a pair of scissors to one of the nuns and asked for them to be boiled. He asked the other nuns to stay. Then he stepped up to Bec, standing very close, his breath stroking her cheek. He spoke softly so only she could hear. 'How long since you delivered a breech?'

'About a year ago. You?'

He shook his head. 'Not since I was a student. You lead, I'll follow.'

He squeezed her shoulder, his confidence trailing through her, reducing her misgivings.

'Melissa.' She touched the woman's shoulder and fixed her gaze on the woman's fear-dilated eyes. 'I need you to listen really carefully. Your baby is coming and it's bottom first. Together we can deliver this impatient imp but you must do what I say, when I say. We're going to need patience and co-operation.'

Melissa nodded, her eyes huge. 'I can do that.'

'Great. First we're going to swing you around so you're lying across the bed. Mark and Tom will have to hold one of your legs each.'

They helped position Melissa so her bottom was on the edge of the bed. One of the nuns sat behind Melissa, cradling her head and supporting her during contractions.

Mark held Melissa's hand, his face pale and dripping with sweat.

'I...want...to...push.' Melissa grunted.

'Go for it.' Bec watched, fingers crossed, hoping the buttocks would deliver with the back uppermost. A swollen scrotum announced the birth of a boy.

It was too early to celebrate.

She gently put her fingers into the vagina. 'His legs are flexed.' Bec spoke out loud, keeping Tom in the picture.

'Pressure behind the knees.'

Tom's quietly spoken words mirrored her thoughts. She gently applied pressure and splinted a leg with her fingers, to draw it down.

'Warm cloths, I need warm cloths.' It seemed outrageous to be demanding warm cloths in the stifling heat but a cold breech could send the cord into spasm and cut off the baby's oxygen supply.

The baby's legs and trunk were delivered and Bec gently held the baby at the hips, keeping his spine uppermost at all times to allow the head to enter the pelvis in the correct position. *Please, don't get stuck.*

'You're doing so well, Melissa.' Bec tried to infuse her words with a sense of calm that she didn't feel. She gently looped some cord down to prevent compression.

She rotated the baby's back from one side to the

other to encourage the arms to gather in a flexed position across the chest as she delivered the shoulders.

'Lovsett manoeuvre—well done.' Tom left his post for a moment and draped the baby in warm cloths. 'I've checked the foetal heart by counting the cord pulsations. He's doing OK.'

Melissa swallowed hard and glanced at Mark. 'It *will* be OK because we're here at this place.'

Bec's heart stalled at the belief in Melissa's voice. The delivery of the head was the hardest and most dangerous part of the breech. She hooked her gaze with Tom's, expecting to find trepidation and dread to match her own.

Instead, respect shone back at her from deep within his eyes. He mouthed, 'You can do this.'

Kneeling on the floor, she straddled the baby's body across her arm, preparing to deliver the head by flexion. With her right fingers flexing the head and her left fingers on the baby's face, she waited for another contraction.

Nothing happened.

Seconds merged into one minute and then another.

'Melissa, your baby needs to be born.' Quiet urgency infused Tom's words. He sat her up, feeling her abdomen for a contraction.

He nodded to Bec. 'Now, Melissa. One big push, *now.*'

'Arrgh!' Melissa pushed, her face puce with effort.

The baby's head slipped through the pelvis as Bec directed it downward and then up over Melissa's abdomen, in a large arc.

Purple and unresponsive, the baby lay completely still on his mother's stomach. *No!*

Tom quickly tied off the cord with suture thread and

cut it with the boiled scissors. He rubbed the baby firmly with the cloth. 'Come on, little guy.' His words sounded loud in the painful silence of the room.

Bec wiped the baby's nose and mouth and tilted the baby downward. 'We don't have anything we can use to aspirate.' She couldn't hide the panic in her voice.

Tom rubbed the sternum and blew on the little boy's face in short, sharp puffs.

The baby's colour deepened to a dusky blue.

Melissa sobbed, gripping Mark's hand.

A feeble cry broke the stifling silence.

Then a louder, more demanding cry rent the air and purple became pink and pink became an indignant red.

'Bless him, he's gloriously grumpy.' Relief poured through Bec as she watched Tom reverently wrap the baby up until all that could be seen was a shock of black hair, enormous black eyes and his indignant wide-open mouth.

Tom as a baby. The thought thudded through her.

Had he looked like this gorgeous baby with his mixed Eurasian heritage? A stabbing pain rocked her. How it must have tortured his mother to have to abandon him to others' care.

Bec turned her attention back to Melissa. The placenta was delivered with a minimum of fuss and the nuns, Bec and Tom cleaned everything up and scrubbed the floors. Melissa's observations were stable and the baby sucked contentedly at his mother's breast.

'Bec, Tom, thank you so much.' Mark pumped Tom's hand and suddenly he encircled Bec in a hug, pulling her tightly against him.

Bec waited for panic to engulf her, the familiar panic that rendered her rigid with fear when unknown men touched her.

It didn't come. Instead, she glowed from bringing a child into the world and completing a family. She hugged him back. 'I'm just so glad it all worked out.'

'But I knew it would. This place protects children,' Melissa's voice broke in. 'Thank you so much. We shall call him Tom and his middle name shall be the same as Bec's surname.'

Tom grinned. 'I've never had a namesake before.'

'You better introduce yourself, then.' Melissa passed the baby back to Tom.

He looked down at baby Tom, now calm from being at his mother's breast. The baby stared back at him.

Bec bit her lip at the sight of a tall, dark-haired, chocolate-eyed doctor tenderly cuddling the small, dark-haired, dark-eyed baby against his broad chest. A baby who perhaps looked a lot like a child of his own would have looked.

Tom as a father. The thought sucked the air from her lungs at the precise moment the chill she'd experienced earlier rushed back in. Only this time it stayed like a cold, hard lump.

She didn't want to think of Tom as a father. He was a colleague and friend. And that was all she wanted, right? Being Tom's friend suddenly became the hardest thing she'd ever agreed to.

Tom and Bec sat sipping tea that the nuns had made for them. A plate loaded with local fruits lay between them.

Tom especially loved the contrast of colours in the dragon fruit—bright pink exterior with a white pulp, symmetrically dotted with fine black seeds.

Bec peeled a green orange. 'I'm so glad that's over. I've never been so scared in my professional life as I was then. I had every breech complication screaming at me in my head.'

'You were sensational.' He toasted her with his glass of tea.

She blushed at his praise, her eyes sparkling with childlike glee. Just like when she'd clapped her hands at the idea of making the incense.

He'd seen flashes of this sort of enthusiasm when he'd first met her. But back then she'd immediately covered up her natural response. Now she no longer hid her joy. A quiver of wonder vibrated inside him. Had he played a role in that? Had his friendship helped her blossom into the women she should have always been if her father and ex-boyfriend hadn't thwarted her growth with their regime of fear?

She picked up some jackfruit. 'You weren't bad yourself. The brain is a wonderful thing, isn't it? Stuff you think you've forgotten comes flooding back.' She stared at him, her violet eyes blazing with the light of a job well done. 'You were with me every step of the way. You have no idea how much that helped me.'

He wanted to sink into those eyes, into that passion she had for life. Embrace it. Embrace her. 'I didn't do that much. It's a shame Rebecca isn't a boy's name.'

She laughed. 'I think Tom Monahan Phillips-Lee is a very respectable name for a boy. He has such a great birth story. He'll grow up being told over and over, "You were born in a Buddhist nunnery." It will go down in the family annals and be a much more exciting story than the sanitised conditions of the French hospital in Ho Chi Minh City.'

She sighed. 'My story was pretty dull. Born at one o'clock on a Saturday afternoon at King Edward Hospital. My parents couldn't even remember what the weather was like.'

'At least you have a story.' The words came out uncensored.

She gazed at him, her voice soft but firm. 'So do you.'

'How do you figure that?' Irritation sizzled inside him at her lack of understanding.

'You're part of history. You arrived in Australia and your parents *chose* you. They saw something in you that opened their hearts.' She leaned forward. 'I bet they told you over and over when you were little the story of how they came to choose you. Why they bypassed other orphans and loved you.'

'Yes, they did.' Her words chafed, their truth diluting his experience. 'But I don't have a *birth* story. I have no idea where I was born.'

'You know you were born in Vietnam, in the south, during a war. I doubt it was a hospital. I like to imagine it was somewhere like this.' She reached out and briefly touched his arm, her eyes full of serenity. 'A peaceful place where your mother found refuge in uncertain times.'

His throat tightened. How had she managed to describe his thoughts? When he'd held baby Tom and stared down into his enormous eyes, which peered at him from under a fuzz of black hair, he'd had a sense of *déjà vu. Crazy thoughts.* 'I think you're having flights of fancy.'

She narrowed her eyes at him. 'You've had the same thoughts. I saw them on your face when you held Tom. You sensed something in his eyes.' She placed her hands over his. 'I think that's fine. If it helps you, believe that.'

He wanted to believe. But he was a scientist and he dealt in facts. He pulled his hands away. 'The reality is probably far removed from this.'

'Or it could be really close.' Her insistent words hammered at him.

His jaw clenched. 'Facts are the only thing that will help.'

She raised her brows. 'I disagree. My imagination helped me to survive in my father's house. If this place helps you then weave it into a set of "possible maybes" for your own birth.'

'Next you'll be going all mystical on me.'

'Hey, you're sounding very Western and we're in Asia.' A cheeky grin streaked across her face. 'I'm going to light some incense before we leave to mark Tom's birth.'

An unfamiliar dreamy look floated in the depths of her eyes. 'He's so cute. I bet you looked a lot like baby Tom when you were born.'

'You going all clucky on me, Bec?' Teasing her was easier than dealing with the strange sensation in his gut when she talked about babies.

She suddenly stiffened. 'No. Motherhood isn't for me. I wouldn't trust a relationship enough to bring a child into it.'

An overwhelming sadness crept through him that

this gorgeous woman had settled on being alone and was not reaching out for what every woman deserved. 'So you're going to hide from relationships because of your parents and one failed attempt when you were an immature girl?'

Her face blanched, her skin tightening over her cheekbones. 'That's pretty rich, coming from you. You're hiding behind all that "commitment" nonsense. You've put your life on hold until you find your mother.'

Indignation surged inside him. 'It takes a lot of energy to search. It wouldn't be fair to any woman when my focus can't be on the relationship.'

Her relentless gaze bored into him. 'And what if you never find your mother?'

Like bullets from a gun, the truth of eight small words shattered his heart. He refused to think about that.

CHAPTER EIGHT

AFTER BEING IN the countryside, the full-on hustle of Hanoi hit Bec like a ton of bricks. They'd flown in from Hué. Now the regional city suddenly seemed like a peaceful, rural village in comparison with chaotic Hanoi.

Their driver abruptly changed lanes, narrowly missing a bicycle so laden with fresh flowers that the woman riding it was barely visible. He then headed south around Hoan Kiem Lake.

Tom stretched, his long arms hitting the ceiling of the vehicle. Deep lines of fatigue surrounded his eyes. 'Won't be long now. It will be good to be home again for a while.' He gave her a grin, his eyes dancing cheekily. 'You can have that bubble bath you wanted.'

She sighed in anticipation. 'I can. And I plan to.' She turned to face him, stifling a giggle, trying to ace him on his friendly flirting. 'So take this as advance warning—the bathroom will be occupied and out of bounds for at least an hour.' She raised her brows. 'And the door will be locked.'

He stroked his chin, deep in contemplation. 'Take as long as you like. I'll be busy.'

'Really?' She'd thought he'd at least take the rest of the day to recover before dealing with outstanding issues tomorrow.

'Yep. This job can't wait. While you're having a bath, I'll be fixing the cracked bathroom window.'

'You devil.' She gave him a gentle push. 'I'll have you know I have industrial-strength bubbles.'

He laughed. 'In that case, I could be up the ladder a long time.'

His arm gently rested across the back of the seat, his fingers barely brushing her shoulder.

She relaxed her head against his arm, a sense of contentment washing through her. She knew his teasing meant nothing and he had no plans to watch her take a bath. She couldn't believe she could exchange banter with a man like this and be safe. But Tom not only made her feel safe but protected. She felt sheltered in his friendship, she enjoyed the fact that with him she could let her guard down and be herself.

So much had changed in a short time. It was hard to comprehend that it had only been five weeks ago that she'd begged him to take her with him on the trip. The cholera outbreak had extended the entire journey by an extra three weeks but now her 'Vietnam orientation' was coming to an end.

Tom had been very quiet on the flight back. An unusual tension seemed to surround him. But she hadn't pushed him about it. She didn't feel like talking, either. Everything was about to change.

The time she'd spent with him in villages dotted across Vietnam had been brilliant. *The best times of your life.*

The unwanted thoughts wove into her, making themselves part of her with their clawing sadness. Today it would all come to an end. Tom would continue with his work and she had to make a decision about how best to use her money.

The dull throb under her ribs kicked into action, its ache becoming painfully familiar. She breathed in deeply, trying to empty her mind. Right now she didn't want to think about any of it.

The driver pulled up outside the ornate iron gates of the villa and quickly unloaded their gear. Tien met them at the door with cold, damp towels and deliciously refreshing iced lemon and lime juice diluted with mineral water.

'Oh, I think I'm in heaven.' Bec smiled at Tien, enjoying the coolness of the towel on her face and hands.

'Tom!' A man with bright red hair, glinting golden in the sunshine, bounded down the curved, terrazzo staircase, his energy filling the room. 'Mate, it's great to see you.' He shook Tom's hand enthusiastically with his right hand and thumped him on the back with his left.

What was it about men and their overwhelmingly physical greetings? Bec almost expected him to finish off the welcome by putting Tom in a headlock.

'Jason. How was the holiday?' Tom extricated his hand from the man's enthusiastic grip.

'Fantastic. Caught up with the rels, and then I rode a 750 cc bike across the Nullarbor and soaked up the space. I didn't realise how much I missed the wide open spaces of Australia or the low population, but after a year in Vietnam, it was the tonic I needed.'

His voice suddenly deepened, its tone becoming serious. 'You should visit the farm soon, Tom. Don't leave it too long.' Without waiting for a reply, he turned quickly and faced Bec, his expression open and questioning.

'Jason, meet Bec Monahan.' Tom made the introductions.

'Ah!' Recognition sparked in his blue eyes. 'You're the nurse with a plan and the money to execute it. We need to talk.' He shot out his hand.

Bec grasped it. 'So you're the Jason Tom suggested I speak to.'

'That's me.' His eyes twinkled with a wicked glint. 'But Tom quickly whisked you off to far-flung places before we could talk.'

'You were in Australia at the time.' Tom's voice came out in an uncharacteristic growl. 'She needed to experience the health issues firsthand before she could make a decision. *That*'s why she came on the trip.'

A flicker of a frown creased Jason's brow as he glanced quickly at Tom before focusing his attention back on Bec. 'I'm very keen to sit down and talk to you in detail about all the projects Health For Life is involved in or wishes to be involved in.' All signs of the Aussie lad had vanished. Jason had his professional, philanthropic hat on, and his sincerity shone through.

Excitement fizzed in her veins. 'I'd really like that. I have a few ideas I want to run by you before I interview other agencies.'

'Fantastic.' He pulled out a palm-top. 'Now—'

Tom interrupted. 'She needs some time to catch her breath, Jason. We've worked flat out for five weeks in rough conditions. Right now we both need some time out. Surely tomorrow would be soon enough to talk.'

Jason's brows rose sharply at Tom's protective tone. 'Actually, I was going to suggest we set a date next week because tomorrow neither of you will be here.'

'What?' Bec and Tom's voices harmonised in surprise.

Jason grinned at them. 'The X-ray machine finally arrived for the provincial hospital in Hon Gin.'

'Sensational!' Tom exclaimed. He turned to Bec, his face alive with exhilaration. 'We've been working toward this for this for a long time. Hon Gin is a coal-mining town, and the streets are literally paved in coal and the air is filled with coal dust.'

Understanding dawned. 'And many locals have pneumoconiosis. But why does that mean we're not going to be here tomorrow?'

'There's going to be an official handing-over ceremony of the machine on Wednesday and the people's committee of the province always like to have a doctor at such an occasion.' Jason tilted his head. 'So that means Tom has to go. In fact, they like a crowd and as you've given your time so generously to Health For Life over the last five weeks, the Health For Life board would like you to accompany Tom to the ceremony.'

It means more time with Tom.

She shook away the unprofessional thought. Accepting the invitation on those grounds was hardly ethical. 'That's very kind of you, but I haven't had anything to do with raising funds for the machine so surely someone else should attend. Wouldn't it be a bit odd for me to be there?'

Jason shrugged. 'No, not at all. We're helping the committee keep face. The more the merrier. We're not a huge organisation and as I've only just got back from leave and the other doctors are busy, it makes sense for the two of you to go.'

She glanced at Tom, trying to gauge how he felt about the idea of her accompanying him, but his face was devoid of all expression. *It's just work, part of the job. Part of his job.*

'You'd really be helping us out,' Jason implored her.

His words eased her guilty pleasure at wanting to spend more time with Tom. After all, it was work, not pleasure.

'Sure. Happy to help.'

'Wonderful. OK, I'd better get back to work and you'll want to do some washing and repack. The driver will pick you both up at 8.30 in the morning.' Jason turned to leave.

'Hang on,' Tom called across the foyer. 'Tomorrow's Tuesday.'

'Didn't you say the ceremony was on Wednesday?' Bec's words collided with Tom's.

Jason spun back, a suppressed smile hovering on his face. 'Part of the thank-you package from the people's committee in Hon Gin was a private overnight cruise on one of the many Halong Bay boats.'

Bec's mouth dried at the thought of being alone on a boat overnight with Tom. Not that she feared him. Not at all. She feared herself. 'But—'

'You have to go.' Jason threw her a stern look. 'It would be extremely rude not to take up the hospitality, and keeping face here is everything.' Then his face split into a wide smile. 'Remember to pack your bathers.' He walked off chuckling.

'Halong Bay is a world heritage listed area, Bec.' Tom's voice broke into her chaotic thoughts. 'Every Vietnamese longs to visit. The scenery is breathtaking.'

She knew it would be. Tom in bathers, his golden chest exposed to sunlight…now, that would be breath-stopping. Dealing with it would be something else entirely.

'Just as well it's a digital camera.' Tom laughed as Bec snapped her camera at yet another one of the three thousand jagged, spectacular limestone karsts, which rose majestically from aquamarine-coloured water. 'I think you'll find you have a hundred photos of much the same thing.'

'Philistine. Besides, everyone needs a photo of the teapot.' She aimed her camera toward the oddly shaped karst with its outcrops of rock that did look like a teapot spout. Then she swung around and took a photo of him, her face alive with excitement.

His body vibrated with heat. She had no idea of the effect she had on him. How he breathed more deeply when she was close, just to get the scent of her. How he created reasons to touch her and made them appear platonic. How the sound of her laughter made everything around him seem brighter, and that her empathy for Vietnam connected her to him like no other person.

The deities were mocking him, sending her into his life now. She deserved a man's love and undivided attention. He couldn't offer her that. And he couldn't ask her for anything else. Friendship was all they had and yet it was nothing like any friendship he'd ever experienced.

The hum of the boat's engine lulled them into a lazy haze of relaxation as they puttered around the karsts, and in and out of small bays.

'I have no idea how the captain knows where he's going. It all looks the same to me.' Bec leaned over the teak railing, breathing out a sigh of satisfaction. 'This is the most amazing place I've ever been to. I love the idea of the legend that a dragon's tail carved out the bays.'

'See over there.' Tom extended his right arm.

'See what?' She peered ahead.

Leaning in close he dropped his left hand onto her shoulder and lifted her right arm to point in the correct direction. 'Look along there, a third of the way up the karst.'

'Oh, I see. Is that a cave where the greenery stops and the grey starts?'

He nodded. 'That's right.' He forced his voice to sound casually friendly even though he desperately wanted to pull her into his chest and trail kisses along the curve of her neck. 'There are vast caves all around this area. They've been used for all sorts of things. The French used them as cool storage for food before export-ing around the world and the Vietnamese used them as training areas and hospitals for wounded soldiers, but the most amazing story of all is that Kublai Khan, the Mongolian emperor, was defeated here, using the high tide and bamboo sticks.'

'That's pretty awesome. So, it's a significant area for

lots of reasons. I read in the guide book that one cave is a temple for fertility.'

'Yeah, but that particular piece of rock where people worship doesn't look anything like a teapot.' He dropped his arm from her shoulder, immediately missing the contact.

A small sampan passed by with a woman and three young children on board. Bec smiled and waved. 'Looks like the fertility cave is doing its job.'

He gave a wry smile. 'There are plenty of kids in Vietnam. We have one of the youngest populations in the world.'

Bec continued waving to the children, her gaze fixed on them. 'What about you? Do you plan to add to the number?'

Her question came out of left field, assaulting his defences. He immediately deflected the question.

'Mum would love to be a grandmother. She's never happier than when she's up to her elbows in play dough, paint and glitter glue.' He laughed. 'She's still working as a kinder assistant to get her fix. Dad teases her but he's just as bad. He enjoys teaching some of the wayward kids woodwork and he gets them down in the milking shed, mucking out. He reckons there's nothing quite like getting kids working with animals to help them see the world in a new light.'

Bec's expression took on a dreamy look. 'I bet your mum baked cakes and helped out in the classroom.' Her voice suddenly dropped in volume. 'And your dad watched you play sport, and insisted on teaching you how to change the tractor oil.'

Somehow she made the ordinary, everyday things of his childhood sound extraordinary. An incredibly clear image of his dad suddenly projected itself into his memory—Dad walking into the kitchen from the milking shed, a broad smile on his weather-beaten face, a billy of creamy milk in one hand and his other hand raised in greeting. An unexpected wave of homesickness rolled through him.

The boat dropped anchor, the rumble of the chain loud in the silence.

'Tom, you avoided answering my question.'

Her firm voice broke into his thoughts. She'd pinned him down and he knew her well enough now to know it was easier to just answer. He shrugged. 'I don't know if I'll have kids. I have no medical history so I could be passing on a genetic illness.'

Her violet eyes flashed with disbelief. 'You're not serious?'

He kept his voice steady, belying the ire that streaked through him. 'Why wouldn't I be serious?'

Concentration lines appeared on the bridge of her nose. 'I understand that as an adoptee you have no idea of your parents' medical history, but many of us don't have much of a clue. My mother died when I was too young to have asked the questions and I was estranged from my father. My aunt has some idea but I have a black hole on my father's side.'

'And doesn't it worry you that you could carry a predisposition to a genetic illness?' He folded him arms across his chest.

'Doesn't it worry you that this boat could sink right now?'

'That's hardly a comparison.' He heard his 'I'm the doctor, I know best' tone. The one that made his mother purse her lips.

Bec raised her brows and matched his crossed-arms stance. 'Yes, it is. You're saying you want certainty but nothing is certain in life. This boat could sink on this trip but you took the trip anyway.'

Her logic chafed like prickly heat. 'Right, so your decision not to have children based on not risking a relationship is more valid than mine based on a lack of scientific data.'

A tremor of tension raced across her shoulders. 'I think you're living your life based on facts, and facts don't always give the true picture. What about the fact you could be giving a child the most wonderful grandparents?'

Frustration bubbled in his veins. He spun away from her. 'Don't romanticise my childhood.'

'Why not? From where I'm standing, it sounds pretty good to me.'

Her words tore at him. Her childhood had been far from good. He turned back. She stood small and determined, her chin jutting forward, her lips plump and firm and her breasts straining against her shirt.

All his indignation fled.

The need to protect clashed with the need to haul her against him and kiss her senseless. *Think friendship.* 'We're spending the day in one of the most beautiful places in the world so why are we disagreeing?'

She wrinkled her nose. 'You're right.'

He feigned surprise. 'Can I have that in writing?'

She rolled her eyes. 'No such luck, but I will concede

that Halong Bay deserves nothing less than harmony and understanding.'

'And swimming.' They needed to have some fun and put their differences aside. 'The crew have taken a picnic over to that little beach you can see. They've left food, towels and kayaks. We've got a few hours while they take a siesta here on the boat.' As he pulled his T-shirt over his head, he talked through the fabric. 'It's a tradition to enter the water from the deck of the boat and swim to the beach.'

He raised his head as he dropped the shirt to the deck. Eyes like large purple pools met his gaze, backlit with swirling emotions.

His solar plexus took a hit. Raw, intense need pounded him as he glimpsed desire emerging from the swirl in her eyes.

She swallowed as a flare of fear darkened her eyes. *Fool.* 'Can't you swim?'

She shook her head. 'Oh, no, I can swim. I'm a good Aussie girl and was dispatched to swimming lessons from the age of five.'

'Great.' He gave her a reassuring smile. 'Well, there's no need to be scared of the jump. I'll go first and demonstrate.' He climbed quickly to the highest point wanting to kick himself that he'd even thought he'd seen desire in her gaze. It had just been fear at the thought of jumping from the deck of a boat into the water.

She's your friend. Nothing more, nothing less.

With an almighty whoop he freed his mind from the jumble of clashing emotions and jumped off the boat. Clutching his knees, he embraced the four-metre drop, bombing into the clear water below.

Salty water encased him, the exhilaration of the jump propelling him again to the surface. He pushed his arms forward and swam around the boat, using the exercise to put his libido back in its box. He rounded the stern and looked up.

Bec stood at the highest point of the boat. Two tiny pieces of blue and pink Lycra were moulded to her body, concealing little and emphasising every delicious curve and contour.

Blood raced around his body. Suddenly the water wasn't anywhere near cold enough.

For weeks she'd hidden her lithe body under baggy trousers and blouses, leaving everything to his imagination. His imagination had failed to do her justice.

Her voice called out, 'What's the water like?'

'Fine.' Had his voice sounded strangled?

'So I just jump?' She peered over the side, nibbling her bottom lip.

His blood pounded faster. Impossibly, even more blood surged to his groin. 'Yep, it doesn't matter that you can't dive, just jump. It's great fun and there's nothing to be afraid of. Enjoy the leap, it's quite cathartic.' He spread his arms out. 'I'm right here when you land and I promise I'll protect you from any lurking dragons.'

'OK.' She elongated the word, her hesitancy clear as her voice trailed off. Leaning forward, she extended her arms high above her head, the action pushing her breasts up and out against the flimsy Lycra.

He gave an internal groan.

She flexed her legs and, rising up on her toes, pushed off the deck, executing a perfect dive.

Mesmerised, he watched her taut hands slice through the water, her body following in superb fluid motion, the dive ending with the tiniest flick of water as her toes disappeared under the surface.

Incredulity tangoed with delight. She continued to amaze him in every way. Who would have thought she could dive like a professional?

Kicking up, she broke the surface, teasing devilment on her face. 'Good dive, was it?'

'You rotter.' He splashed her and tried to sound indignant as laughter shook him. 'Here I was being all chivalrous, a knight in shining armour, promising to slay dragons and rescue you if you needed it, and you took advantage of my good nature.'

She grinned. 'Sorry, I couldn't resist it. I also had years of diving lessons. I shall restore your honour.' She flailed her arms about and slipped back under the water for a moment and then rose out again. Passing her hand across her forehead, she feigned distress. 'Oh, gallant sir, please help a maiden in distress.' She gasped overdramatically then disappeared again under the water.

Joining in the fun, he dived under the water. Slipping his left arm around her waist, he pulled her toward him, holding her back tightly against his chest.

They broke the surface together, her body wriggling deliciously against his, sending sparks of need shuddering through him.

She trod water, giggling and started to pull away from him, her hand against his forearm. 'You are too kind, sir. Thank you for rescuing me.'

Two could play at this game. He whispered against her ear, 'I haven't finished rescuing you yet.'

'Oh.' The word came out on a breath as she stiffened slightly, before completely relaxing against him, her legs tangling with his.

It scared him to think about how good it felt to have her in his arms. He assumed the rescue position, his left arm holding her head above water and his right arm propelling them toward the tiny strip of sand.

His feet touched sand and he stood up in water up to his chest. He swung her around to face him, his arms loosely circling her waist.

She tilted her head and raised her brows. 'I didn't know knights could swim. I thought they were pretty useless without their horses and their swords.'

'Careful.' His arms tightened around her, pulling her gently toward him, holding her body against his. Her length lined his and her ankles twined around his calves. 'Cheeky maidens can be thrown back.' His voice came out low and hoarse.

Humour danced in her eyes. 'I apologise most sincerely.' Laughing, she hooked his gaze and suddenly all traces of fun vanished, replaced with a look so serious it seared him. She gazed up at him, her eyes dark violet, shimmering brightly with undisguised need. Tiny droplets of water clung to the tips of her thick brown lashes, and a pulse fluttered at the base of her throat.

It took every ounce of willpower not to flick the droplets off with his tongue.

'Thank you for rescuing me, Tom.'

She spoke softly, the sound evaporating so quickly it was almost as if the words had not been said. But the echo of the message resonated loud and clear, vibrating in his chest.

Tilting her head forward, she pressed her lips gently against his cheek.

The touch was brief, a light caress. But the softness and warmth of her lips sent a riot of sensation ricocheting through him, making every part of him vibrate with suppressed longing.

She trusts me. The warning sounded faintly in the recesses of his mind.

She wants me. Need dominated.

Weeks of concealed emotions exploded inside him, pushing every rational thought from his head. He couldn't hold back any longer. He needed her arms around his neck, her legs around his waist, her lips against his own. He needed her now like he needed air.

For the first time in forever he was living for the moment. Taking what was on offer, no questions asked.

Bec's lips tingled, deliciously grazed from the stubble on Tom's cheeks. She looked up into eyes alive with a smoking desire that matched her own.

Had she been standing on the sand she would have melted against him, her legs unable to hold her.

His desire-filled gaze swirled with tumbling emotions. Adoration and reverence emerged, penetrating deep into her soul, warming all of her, releasing parts of her she'd locked away. Freeing her. This amazing man had rescued her, opened her world and taught her to trust again.

This man she loved.

The thought rocked her through to her toes. She loved him. *Oh, God, she loved him.*

She waited for the fear to grip her heart.

She braced herself, waiting for all the reasons to flood her brain and tell her why this was a bad idea.

She waited for the overwhelming urge to flee.

None came.

Instead, peace and tranquility, linked with a sense of belonging, slid through her.

This was right. This time, with this man, she'd got it right. This man who was her friend, her confidant and her mentor. Her partner, the future father of longed-for children.

She wanted him. She wanted to mesh this amazing psychological bond they shared with a physical one.

She lifted her head up, greeting his lips as he slanted his mouth across hers. Tenderness, mixed with a restrained firmness sent shuddering ribbons of wonder swirling through her.

Her heart cried out in joy. He was waiting for her to tell him she wanted him, too.

She flicked her tongue against his lips. He tasted of salt. Of heat. Of thundering need—all the flavours she knew he would taste on her. She plunged her fingers into his thick hair and opened her mouth to his.

His restraint fell away and with a groan he plundered her mouth, taking what she offered him. His tongue explored, each flicking caress spiralling her need for him higher and higher.

His arms tightened around her—lust simmering with

tenderness. He drew her so closely against him that not even water separated them.

It wasn't close enough.

She felt him hard against her thigh. A thrill of secret power shot through her that she could do this to him. Her nipples responded, firming into peaks, pressing against his chest, tingling and tight. Aching. Aching for his touch.

His mouth moved from hers, trailing kisses along her neck and up along her ear. Butterfly-light kisses with pinpoint accuracy. Each kiss zeroed in, showering her in waves of quivering shivers.

Glorious sensation racked her. She threw back her head, her shoulders following, letting him and the water support her. Begging for him to extend his wondrous touch.

'You're completely stunning, Bec.' His deep voice pulsated through her. 'You've hidden amazing treasure under baggy clothing. I've spent hours fantasising about what you look like naked, and the reality will far exceed expectation.'

'Really?' The needy girl inside her rose up.

His gaze, hot and simmering, burned into hers. 'Believe it.' He pushed the Lycra aside, his thumb grazing a breast in decreasing circles, the touch bringing pleasure and exquisite pain exploding in mini-bursts all through her body.

Despite being in the water, fire raced across her skin, her breath becoming ragged gasps. She'd never been touched like this before, with such reverence. Such adoration.

He groaned and lowered his mouth, covering her breast, his tongue flicking slowly at her nipple before giving in to his hunger for her and taking it into his mouth.

Showers of silver light reined down on her. Her body took over from her brain, taking her into another realm, completely centred on the glorious sensations that streaked through her.

She bucked against him, the throbbing deep within her crying out for his touch. She moved to touch him, wanting to feel her hands in his hair, have her lips explore his face, but his hand slid between her legs, driving out every thought, blanking her mind.

He cupped her.

Sensation ruled. Need conquered.

She pushed against his hand, desperate for pressure, quivering to be filled. She raised her head.

'Stay and enjoy, I want to give this to you.' His silken voice stroked her.

Just like his hand. His fingers traced her slickness, wet with water, wet with longing. She should have felt exposed and vulnerable. But she felt safe and treasured.

Every barrier she'd built in eight years crumbled to dust. She gave herself up to him completely. Opening herself up to the sheer bliss of his touch.

Gentle, long, shallow strokes reduced her limbs to liquid muscle. Each tantalising caress slowly deepened, bringing her core to fever pitch, driving her higher and higher and higher until pleasure morphed with pain and the temptation of release taunted her.

Shuddering, she clenched against his fingers as his thumb circled her.

Reality receded. Sensation consumed her.

Colours exploded in her head as a cry of release left her throat.

A deliciously languid feeling rolled through her as her mind slowly came back to the present. Strong arms cradled her to a broad chest and she laid her head on Tom's shoulders. 'Thank you.'

His eyes, thick with desire, stared down at her. 'You're welcome.'

'That was incredible. I had no idea it could feel like that.' She trailed her forefinger across his chest, enjoying the dips and rises of toned muscle, and slowly snaked a path downward. 'I think I could perhaps return the favour on the beach.'

He gripped her harder. 'If you want me to walk to the beach, you'd better stop your hand's adventures right now.' His voice rasped.

She laughed, overjoyed that her touch could wield so much influence. Reluctantly she moved away from him. 'I'll race you to shore. This time I might just win.'

She ducked under the water in a shallow dive and swam the short distance until the length between her and the sand was only a few centimetres. She ran out of the water toward the picnic rug all set out for them. She bent down, quickly grabbing the rug, and ran toward a secluded area, surrounded by trees.

'Gotcha.' Tom's hand gently closed around her upper arm.

She turned straight into his arms, melding her mouth to his. Together they fell to the rug. Hands tore at bathers until they were skin on skin. Need meeting need.

'I need you now,' his hoarse voice implored.

She gloried in his words. 'I need you, too.' Cupping his jaw with her hands, keeping her gaze riveted to his, she lowered herself over him. Glorifying in the fire of the stretch as she filled herself with him. Moulding herself to him. Claiming him as hers.

Ecstasy played across his face as she rose with him. With gazes fused, they drove each other closer and closer toward the precipice. Together they dived into the glorious vortex, shattering simultaneously, re-forming as one.

CHAPTER NINE

'HEY!' TOM DUCKED as Bec cracked open a cooked crab and fluid sprayed down his arm.

'Sorry. Crabs are a lot of effort for little return, aren't they?' She was nestled between his legs and together they were eating their way through an enormous seafood meal.

She turned her head slightly and flicked out her tongue, trailing a line along his biceps, licking the errant moisture from his skin. 'Oh, you taste all salty.' She giggled, leaning back against him and looking up into his face.

Heat slammed him. 'I imagine you do, too. Perhaps I should find out.' He leaned down and kissed her, unable to resist the touch and taste of those tempting lips. He felt cocooned in time. Cocooned in Halong Bay, as if they were the only two people who existed in the world.

He released her mouth. 'Just as I thought—salty. But I might have to do some more research.'

She laughed and leaned forward toward the food, this time shelling the most enormous prawns he'd ever seen.

For three hours they'd had this tiny beach to themselves. They'd spent their time swimming, eating and just enjoying being together. *And the best sex you've ever had in your life.*

Their lovemaking had been exhilarating and intense. He thought his frantic, consuming need to possess her would have been sated after they'd made love, but it hadn't gone away. Instead, it had evolved into something different, less wild, more defined, more real. He longed to make love to her slowly, to fully explore her in the comfort of a bed. He wanted to know what stirred her, what would cause her to yearn for his touch, and what made her reach for him.

He'd never experienced anything like it with any other woman. The craving to constantly touch her burned strongly—a hand on her shoulder, an arm around her waist, his lips on her hair—and he'd kept her close to him ever since they'd fallen back on the picnic rug, exhausted but replete.

'Tom, look over there.' Bec pointed to the sky.

Black clouds bore down on the white fluffy ones that scudded across the sky. 'Rain coming. We better head back. Do you want to swim or go in the basket boat?'

She gave a wry smile. 'It's a moot point whether a trip in the basket boat is really more like a swim. Besides, I've eaten so much, I think I could do with the exercise.' She stood up, stretched and rubbed her belly.

His desire for her, always simmering inside him, boiled over at the sight of her fingers splayed against her rounded belly. He pulled her to him. 'I've got an idea of how we could exercise.'

Her eyes deepened to a purple hue. 'Is that so?'

'Mmm.' He dipped his head to her neck, kissing her,

sucking her skin into his mouth as the overpowering urge to mark her as his hit him. 'After all, it's going to be raining.'

A wicked grin danced across her face. 'So we'd need to exercise indoors.'

'I was thinking behind closed doors. My cabin door.' He extended his kisses as she tilted her head back. 'After I've washed all that salt water off you in the shower.'

He heard her moan, the sound thrilling him to his marrow.

She spun out of his arms and jogged to the water's edge calling over her shoulder, 'Don't be too long or I'll have used all the hot water.' She splashed into the water and dived in.

He followed, chasing a promise.

She outswam him and five minutes later he hauled himself up the steep steps into the stern of the boat. He strode up the long, narrow corridor, water streaming off him. Pushing open his cabin door, he expected to be greeted by the sound of running water.

Silence.

The bed lay empty and so did the bathroom. Confused, he turned and headed back out into the corridor. He met Bec fully clothed again in her Vietnamese gear, her brow creased in concern. She clutched the medical backpack. The transformation from siren to nurse was startling. The only hint of their time on the beach was her wet hair.

Disappointment slugged him.

'The cook has sliced his hand badly with the carving knife. I've bound it but we need your stitching prowess.'

He stared at her, his brain slowly computing as his libido receded.

She smiled at him like he was a child. 'You might want to grab a towel and meet me up on deck.'

Everything fell into place. 'Right. Yes, of course. I'll be up there in a minute.' He watched her walk along the corridor. He imagined he had X-ray vision, seeing straight through the utilitarian cotton to the shapely buttocks moving seductively underneath. Right now, his imagination was as close as he was going to get.

He quickly shucked his board shorts, towelled himself dry and pulled on his clothes. Taking three steps at a time, he bounded up to the top deck. In the main living area he found the six crew members all hovering around Bec and a young man whose pale face told him he was the patient. He was almost as white as the bandage around his hand.

Bec glanced up at him as he walked in, her welcoming smile lighting up her face. The same smile she'd given him each time she'd seen him, the same smile she'd bestowed on him for the past few weeks. Today it looked the same, but it felt very different.

He watched her as she unwrapped the bandage. Her aura of competence and friendliness surrounded her, but it lacked the tension that had always been part of her. He suddenly realised that for the first time since he'd met her, she was completely and utterly relaxed.

She wrinkled her nose. 'I tried to explain stitches to Trang but my Vietnamese didn't come close.' She gave an embarrassed laugh. 'I think my charades just scared him.'

'No worries. I think my Vietnamese is up to this.'

Tom smiled at the youth, greeting him before examining the wound. 'It's deep. He's cut into muscle.'

'I thought so.' Bec opened the dressing pack and drew up some local anaesthetic, pre-empting his request. As usual, she was organised and efficient.

Tom changed to Vietnamese. 'How did you cut your hand, Trang?' He sat down and applied more pressure to the wound.

'I don't know. I didn't feel it. I just saw the cut.' Beads of sweat clustered on his forehead.

'A sharp knife is a dangerous thing.' Tom checked the edges of the wound.

'But it isn't very sharp. It wasn't cutting well.'

Bec leaned over his shoulder, her chest brushing his back. 'It's a pretty jagged cut. How did it happen?'

Tom peered more closely at the gash. 'He said the knife wasn't sharp and he didn't feel the cut which really doesn't make a lot of sense.'

Trang's face paled as he suddenly leaned forward, heaving.

Bec grabbed a bucket and pushed it into his hands just as he started to vomit.

'Lucky save.' Tom smiled his thanks. Her quick actions had just prevented him being covered in Trang's stomach contents.

A dreamy look crossed her face. 'It's my lucky day.'

The softly spoken words wafted around him warmly, but settled on him uncomfortably. He shrugged the feeling away. Pressing a finger around the wound, he asked Trang, 'Does it hurt here…here…here?'

The patient shook his head. 'No, it doesn't really feel.'

'Pass me a needle please, Bec.' This didn't make sense. He should have a throbbing hand. He should have felt the cut.

'Here you go. What are you thinking? Some sort of paraesthesia? Perhaps he cut a nerve.'

Tom unsheathed the needle and pressed it around the hand. 'Tell me when you feel a sharp jab.'

'No, I don't feel. My feet are tingling, too.' Trang slumped at the table as he heaved again.

Bec passed the young man water to rinse his mouth and then mopped his brow with a cool cloth. 'I know he could be vomiting from shock but do you think he might have cut his hand because he was feeling unwell and lost concentration?'

Tom shrugged. 'The symptoms are pretty confusing. I'm going to stitch the hand first. That might turn out to be the easy bit. Can you do a set of observations?'

'Sure.' Bec picked up the sphygmomanometer and wrapped it around Trang's upper arm.

As Tom injected the local anaesthetic into Trang's already numb hand he started to sort the symptoms in his head. Nausea, vomiting, sweating, numb hand, tingling feet. On the surface it could be, as Bec had said, a vaso-vagal reaction. But he had a nagging feeling that if he went with that, it would be the easy diagnosis. 'Now I am going to stitch your hand.'

Trang gave a feeble nod. 'Jus doit.' His words ran together in a slur.

'Tom, his blood pressure is really low.' Bec's questioning and concerned gaze fixed on him. 'Food poisoning?'

Tom threaded the curved needle and started to bind the muscle layers of the hand together in a series of small stitches. 'Maybe.' Without looking up, he asked the other crew. 'Does anyone feel sick or dizzy?'

'I don't know what you just asked them, Tom, but they're all shaking their heads.'

'I think we just ruled out food poisoning.' He changed over to the finer thread for the skin closure stitches.

Bec encouraged Trang to drink some more water. 'Not necessarily. Trang's the cook. He could have tasted dinner as he prepared it and the contamination could be from that. We're well because we haven't eaten that meal yet.'

He smiled at her logic as he snipped the thread. 'Very perceptive.' Keen intelligence wrapped up in a delicious body. It was a powerful combination. One he couldn't wait to explore again. And he would as soon as he'd solved the Trang puzzle.

The sick man took a sip of water but most of it dribbled out of his mouth.

'He's dribbling, Tom.' Apprehension clung to her words.

'And he's slurring his speech.' He quickly finished the last stitch, his brain frantically searching his memory for clues. 'Trang, is your mouth feeling numb?'

'My mouf an' my tong.' The words sounded thick.

'Squeeze my hand as hard as you can.' Tom placed his hand against Trang's uninjured hand.

The pressure was weak. Far too weak for a young man of twenty.

Bec's words about tasting a meal rang in his head. 'What were you cooking?'

The young man's gaze slid away. 'Soup.'

A red flag hoisted itself in his mind. 'What sort of soup? It's important you tell me. You could be very, very sick.'

Trang threw an imploring look at his captain and then dropped his head. 'Puffer fish.'

All the symptoms dropped into place. He'd been cooking the delicacy that the Vietnamese government was actively discouraging. Discouraging because *fugu* was deadly. 'Bec, you were right. He's poisoned himself with his cooking. He's got tetrodotoxin poisoning.'

A stunned look passed across her face. 'But that's a neu-rotoxin and it will slowly paralyse his respiratory system. We're hours from the mainland. Hours from a respirator.'

'I know, but he said he was making soup. Let's hope the fish had been gutted and that there were only traces of toxin heavily diluted by water.' He turned to the now frightened young man. 'How did you prepare the fish?'

'I took out the guts. I know these are where the poison is.'

Tom sighed. 'Did you boil the heads and skin?'

Trang sobbed. 'I did.'

'There's no antidote, is there?' Bec bit her bottom lip.

'No. None. It paralyses the victim, leaving them fully conscious. A living death.' He stood up and gave Trang's shoulder a squeeze. 'He cooked the eyes of the puffer fish, which are full of the toxin. But we've got charcoal to absorb it and if we can give him a gastric lavage and empty his stomach we have a fighting chance.'

Bec started rummaging through the medical kit. 'I guess we can use the IV tubing as a lavage tube.'

'Good thinking. All we can do is address the symptoms. Let's hope that this is as bad as he gets.' He touched her arm. 'I'll tell the captain to head the boat back to Halong City.'

She nodded, a flash of regret streaking across her face. He knew exactly how she felt. It was going to be a long night but not the type of long night they'd both imagined.

Bec woke with a start. Rain pounded the porthole as the boat rocked violently. Her stomach lurched and she dragged in a deep breath, trying to calm the seasickness. Tom had sent her to bed. His bed. Only problem was, he wasn't in it.

Just as she'd finished the gastric lavage and charcoal treatment, the storm had hit. The tranquil sea she'd swum in only a few hours before had become a roiling, churning mass of white-capped waves, thudding hard against the hull of the boat, making it roll back and forth. Making her stomach roll. Just like on the motorbike when she'd succumbed to motion sickness. Tom had taken one look at her and ordered her to bed.

She lay staring at the inky blackness outside, guilt nibbling at her. She wondered how Trang was doing. She should get up and help Tom. Sitting up, she edged to the side of the bed and then stood. The boat lurched. She fell back as acid burned the back of her throat. She hated this. Hated feeling this weak.

She lay down again and closed her eyes. The sound of the doorhandle being pulled down made her turn over. Tom's bulk filled the small cabin. Wondrous delight wound through her. She could lie and watch him for hours. 'How's Trang?'

He sat on the edge of the bed, his weight tilting her toward him. His long fingers stroked her temple. 'He's stable. And damned lucky. His decision to make soup saved his life as it diluted the toxins. He hasn't deteriorated and his breathing is OK. The first three hours are the most dangerous and we're into four now. He's improved slightly.'

'Thank goodness. I'm sorry I let you down.'

His hand cupped her cheek. 'You didn't let me down. You were there when I needed you. The last couple of hours have just been observation. He's being monitored by one of the crew who will come and get me if anything changes.' He kicked off his shoes. 'How are you feeling?'

'Fine as long as I stay lying down.' She put her hand over his. 'You look worn out.'

'Yeah.' He tried to stifle a yawn. 'Is there room for me in there?'

'Absolutely.' She moved over to make some space.

He lay down next to her, drawing her back against his front, moulding his body to hers and wrapping his strong arms around her in a tender hug. He gently kissed her hair and sighed, his arms tightening around her.

She breathed out and snuggled in, sheltering in his caring arms, feeling the rise and fall of his chest against her back. Serenity flowed through her. She belonged here with this amazing, caring man. When she'd come to Vietnam with a plan to help, she'd never thought that Vietnam would give her a greater gift. The gift of trust.

His breathing slowed, and his body slackened

against her. She stroked his arms. The poor guy was exhausted. She smiled, thinking about their vigorous lovemaking and swimming hours earlier. She'd been part of wearing him out.

When he'd made love to her she'd never been so exhilarated in her life. It was as if he'd opened a door to a new world and she'd tumbled through it into paradise. And it was so much more than the sex.

The sex had been brilliant but lying here in his arms feeling cosseted and treasured, was part of this new world. A world of trust and respect, of friendship and understanding, and infinite caring. Of love.

Love.

For the first time in her life she recognised what love in its true form really was. She could touch it and taste it and feel it.

She belonged with this man.

With her legs entwined with his and her arms resting against his, she drifted into sleep.

Tom quietly let himself back into the cabin. He'd woken and gone up to check Trang. He was much the same but it could take five days for the paresthaesia and muscle weakness to subside completely. They were still an hour away from berthing in Halong City and the blinding rain and wind hadn't abated.

He should wake Bec up but she looked so peaceful, lying there. He half reclined next to her, stroking her hair from her face. She cuddled into him, her head resting on his chest.

What a night. She'd been sick and he'd been so exhausted he'd barely been able to stand. No languid love-making. Just sleep. He'd been surprised at how deep his few hours of sleep had been. Usually he tossed and turned when he was overtired and on call.

She stirred, murmuring in her sleep. He thought he heard his name.

She'd cried out his name yesterday. Memories of her passionate and generous lovemaking on the beach flooded through him. She'd given herself to him completely and utterly with an intensity that had stunned him.

No barriers.

No guarding.

She'd been open in a way she'd never been before. It was as if he'd discovered a new Bec.

She opened her eyes. 'Morning.'

'Morning.' He looked down into crystal-clear violet eyes. Eyes completely free of all the shadows that had been a permanent part of her. Eyes whose new clarity no longer hid her emotions but emphasised them.

Eyes that shone with love.

Oh, God. His breath rushed out of his lungs so fast it was as if he'd been king-hit in the solar plexus. She loved him. How could he have been so stupid? So careless?

Thank you for rescuing me.

He threw his head back, closing his eyes against the ache that burned inside him. He'd ignored the warning voices in his head and given in to lust, taking everything she'd offered and kidding himself she'd had the same overwhelming needs as him. Thinking it had just been sex.

A tight band crushed his chest. Breathing got hard.

But this was Bec.

Bec, who'd never known true friendship before. Bec who'd been hurt so badly in the past that there would be no way she would have given herself so totally to him without love.

Reality crashed over him like the violent waves in Halong Bay. She loved him.

He didn't love her.

How could he love anyone when he had this empty space eating away inside him, and no knowledge about who he really was?

Nausea poured through him. His heart pounded in his chest. Sweat broke out on his brow. The cabin suddenly seemed small and stifling.

Trust me, Bec.

Self-loathing poured through him. He'd just hurt the one person in the entire world he'd tried to heal and protect.

CHAPTER TEN

SLEEP VANISHED INSTANTLY as the smile on Tom's face contorted to a painful grimace. Bec sat up, immediately on full alert. 'Are you OK? You look really pale.'

He lifted her off his chest and slid off the bed, keeping his back to her. 'Fine. I'm fine. You need to get up and get ready.'

A shiver of cold ran through her. Yesterday he hadn't been able to keep his hands off her. This morning it was as if she was noxious. *Don't be ridiculous. This is Tom.*

He started shoving his few clothes into his backpack. 'We're docking really soon. I'll take Trang to the hospital and then I have to go to the X-ray ceremony. I have to be back in Hanoi by tonight.'

The streaks of cold froze inside her. 'Hang on. What's this "*I* have to go to the ceremony". Shouldn't that be "*we*"?'

His shoulders stiffened. 'Yes. Sorry. I'm just used to doing things on my own.' He tossed her clothes to her, his face a blank mask. 'Please, get dressed.'

She pulled the trousers and blouse over her underwear, gaining much-needed dignity as well as clothing.

She stood up on wobbly legs as the boat continued to pitch. 'Tom, what's going on?'

Pain slashed his face. 'I'm sorry, Bec.'

The words ripped through her, leaving a trail of bleeding destruction in every part of her. Her mind battled her body, not wanting to believe the change in him. There *must* be a reason. 'Sorry for what, Tom?' *Please, don't say yesterday.*

'Yesterday. I'm sorry for yesterday.'

Her legs gave way and she sat on the bed, her hands gripping the edge of the mattress. 'Exactly which bit of yesterday are you sorry for?'

The skin tightened across his high cheekbones, taut with tension. 'I shouldn't have made love to you.'

Her heart shuddered. She swallowed hard, trying to keep her mind clear, not letting her pain swamp her. 'Why not? We're consenting adults.'

Deep furrows scored his brow. 'Yes, but I think you've attached more to it than just a romp in the sand.'

He knew she loved him.

Bile scalded the back of her throat. Her body shivered uncontrollably. Wrapping her arms around herself, she threw her head up and stared into eyes that projected sympathy overlaid with guilt. She forced her words out against a constricted throat. 'And you haven't attached anything to it?'

Remorse blazed across his face. 'No. I can't attach anything to it. I can't love you.'

Her heart shattered, searing her with burning pain. She'd trusted him. Trusted him with her story, with her friendship. Like every other man she'd known, he'd taken her trust and discarded it, as if it had no value. It was as if she'd put her hand up and said, 'Use me.'

She gasped for breath as blackness swirled in her mind. Why, after eight years, had she dropped her guard and opened herself up for this? *Stupid, stupid girl*.

Men could not be trusted. Men abused. Men took. Men…

No!

This is Tom.

From the moment he'd met her he'd looked out for her. He'd insisted she pace herself workwise, he'd quietly cared for her in so many ways. He'd held her when she'd been sick, had been outraged by her father, and he'd offered her unconditional friendship. He was the most caring, gorgeous man she knew.

Yesterday he'd looked into her soul, his eyes full of reverence and adoration. Pure lust did not look like that. She had *not* been mistaken. There had been far more to it than just a romp in the sand.

So why was he denying that? Why was he was acting like a jerk? None of this made sense. She frantically gathered the shards of her dignity and her self-worth, forcing them together so she could get to the bottom of this and fight for something worth saving. Show *him* they had something worth saving.

She breathed in deeply asking the hardest question of her life. 'Why can't you love me?'

He spun away from her, aching inside, hating himself for putting her through this. 'You know why.'

'No, I don't think I do know why. Please, explain it to me.' Pride carried the words around the cabin.

He jerkily pulled the drawstring on his pack. 'My life is complicated. I've told you that.'

'I think you're making it way more complicated than it needs to be.'

Each softly spoken word pierced him, hammering at everything he knew about himself. He turned to face her. She sat pale, calm and implacable, her chin jutting forward in her familiar and determined way.

He needed her to understand. Needed her to forgive him. 'Half of me is missing. I can't love anyone when I'm not complete myself.'

Her nostrils flared. 'Half of you is *not* missing. You're all here. You are the sum of your biological and adopted parents. Your birth parents gave you great DNA and your Australian parents gave you love and values. You've been blessed, Tom Bracken.'

Anger flared at her dismissal of his feelings. 'I have a family out there somewhere that I don't know. A heritage that is vacant.'

She didn't flinch at his exasperation. Large eyes stared him down. 'No one's life is perfect. No one's parents real or imaginary, ever live up to expectations, Tom. You've woven a dream around a family you want to find. But you also have a loving family in Australia you haven't seen in two years. You have a heritage with them. A family history. Don't turn your back on all that for a pipe dream.'

Resentment coiled in his gut as her words gnawed at him. 'You don't know what you're talking about. I haven't turned my back on my parents. Hell, they encouraged me to come here and work and to look for my mother.'

A sad smile of understanding tugged at her lips. 'Of course they did. They love you and want to support you. They can see you're struggling and they want you to find some peace.'

He snorted in derision. 'Peace. How can I have peace when I don't know if I'm Australian or Vietnamese? When I feel disconnected, no matter where I am?'

A wry expression crossed her face. 'Hey, you don't have to be adopted to feel disconnected or to have a million what-if questions about your life.

'And why do you have to be one or the other? You're both. You belong in both countries. If your mother hadn't given you up and you'd been raised in Vietnam, you would have all these same questions about your dead father. You'd feel more Vietnamese but know part of you was Western. Either way, you're a blend of East and West. Embrace it.'

He wanted to put his hands over his ears, like a child refusing to listen. 'That's too easy. My life can't be reduced to a simple equation.'

Her eyes flashed. 'I don't think you have any idea of what you really have. You've been so lucky.'

Her words hammered him. 'Lucky? My mother abandoned me.' He heard the despair in his voice.

She stood up, her gait rolling with the tossing boat, and walked over to him. 'Your mother gave you up because she loved you more than she loved herself. She gave you up so you could live.'

She put her hand on his arm, her heat seeping into him like water into parched ground. 'War changes all the rules. You were starving, you might have been sick with cholera and the orphanage was your only chance at survival.

'Life is a lottery, Tom. You have to make the best of what you've got. I got dud parents. You got stellar parents. I fought to leave my father and you're fighting to find your mother. But you've been surrounded by love all your life. Don't turn your back on it by putting your life on hold. You once told me to stop hiding and take a chance on an adult relationship. I have. Now I'm asking you to take a chance with me. I'm here and I love you.'

He hated her logic. Hated it that her words dredged up all the thoughts that plagued him every day. He shrugged off her touch, needing distance. 'I'm actively searching for my birth mother. Just because I don't love you doesn't mean my life is on hold.'

She recoiled for a moment as his words had struck her like bullets. 'I think you're using this search for your mother as an excuse to hold people at bay. I think you're scared.'

'Don't be ridiculous.' He snapped the plastic clasps on his backpack with more force than necessary. 'What on earth would I have to be scared about?'

Her look of pitying understanding made his stomach lurch.

She hauled in a breath. 'I think you're scared that Vietnam hasn't given you the sense of completeness that you believed it would, and you feel guilty for missing Australia.' She laced her fingers together. 'You've told yourself for so long that you can't fall in love until you find your birth mother and find the answers to all your questions about yourself. If you admit that you love me then you've just admitted that your search for your mother is over. And that scares the hell out of you.'

His heart pounded, threatening to expose his worst fears and strip him bare. He had to stop this conversation. He had to put an impenetrable distance between them. Had to stop her from ever thinking they could be together.

'Bec, I never promised you love. I only ever offered you friendship. We don't have a future together. I'm sorry you read more into it than I can give.'

A stillness settled over her. Only her eyelashes moved against her cheeks as she blinked furiously. 'I'm a very perceptive reader, Tom.'

The words hung between them.

He blocked them out.

Suddenly she squared her shoulders as the muscles in her throat contracted hard and fast. 'You taught me to trust again and to love. Now you need to take your own lesson and allow yourself to love. But it's your choice and only you can make that decision. I refuse to plead for your love.'

She walked unsteadily to the door. 'I promised Jason I would be part of the X-ray ceremony. The moment that's over I'll leave you to your life.' She stepped out into the corridor, the door closing behind her.

Silence.

His breath shuddered out of his lungs and he sat down hard on the bed. His words had worked. She'd gone. He'd got exactly what he'd wanted. What he'd needed.

He closed his eyes against the image of her face.

The familiar empty space inside him, the space that had been a part of him since he'd been fifteen, abruptly expanded.

Bec stared out the window of the meeting room at the Hon Gin hospital and shuddered. Violent winds bent the coconut trees sideways and blinding rain lashed the buildings. Brown water covered the grounds of the hospital, flooding the gardens. She'd never seen rain or wind like it.

Hin joined her. 'It's the edge of a typhoon.'

His matter-of-fact voice surprised her. 'A typhoon? Shouldn't we have the windows boarded up?'

He smiled at her. 'No, this is not bad. It is not predicted to come this way. The wind should not get any stronger.'

Bec wrapped her arms around herself as a small tree became uprooted. 'Well, that's reassuring.'

Hin smiled, completely missing the irony in her voice.

The rain had only increased the humidity and she dripped in her dress. Due to the importance of the occasion she couldn't wear her Vietnamese farming clothes so she was back in Western clothing. It felt odd to have her legs and arms exposed.

'We're required on the podium now,' Tom's stern voice commanded her from behind.

All traces of affection had faded from his voice. He'd retreated behind the persona of the serious doctor. She closed her eyes and breathed in deeply before she turned to face him. To face the man she loved.

The man who couldn't love her back.

Unbearably, her heart tore a little more.

She just had to get through the next six hours. In six hours she would be back in Hanoi. Alone. Only then could she collapse in a flood of tears and give in to her raw and bleeding grief. But right now she was on show and dignity was her only defence.

She walked to the podium flanked by Hin and Tom and took her seat. Hin placed himself between her and Tom. She looked out onto a sea of colour, of flowing fabrics and complex embroidery. Most women wore the *ao dai,* the graceful and flowing national dress of Vietnam, marking the importance of the occasion. The men wore utilitarian black trousers and white shirts.

Everyone rose to their feet. The Australian flag was hoisted with appropriate pomp and ceremony, taking its place next to the vivid red Vietnamese flag with its central golden star.

The speeches started and Hin translated in a low voice. She took a quick glance sideways at Tom, knowing he had planned to make a short speech in Vietnamese, knowing he'd worried about getting it right. He stared straight ahead through eyes surrounded by deep lines. His shoulders were straight, rigid with tension, while his hands balled into fists and rested on his thighs.

Hands that had caressed her with such tenderness just yesterday.

A lifetime ago.

She sighed. This was all too hard. She would have given anything to hire a driver and go straight to Hanoi. Bypass this excruciatingly public event where they had to be seen together.

But no matter what had happened between them her plans for financing a programme with Health For Life hadn't changed. Part of her belonged in Vietnam. Children like little Minh needed her.

Falling in love with Tom had forced her to acknowledge her desire for a child. Surely *one* good thing could come out of this mess. She'd go to Danang tomorrow and make enquiries about adopting Minh.

Tom's chair scraped against the wooden floor as he rose to give his speech. People in the audience nodded their approval as his deep voice rang out clear and loud, the Vietnamese words flowing from his mouth without a moment's hesitation.

For a few moments applause drowned out the sound of the rain.

A lump formed in Bec's throat and she blinked. Nothing in her life had been as hard as right now, watching Tom from a distance and not being able to share this moment of accolade with him.

A children's choir sang, their voices sweet and high, their red neck scarfs bright against their white school shirts.

Hin leaned over. 'Now they want us to go and see the first X-ray being taken.'

She nodded numbly and followed the dignitaries off the podium, Tom ahead of her in deep discussion with the chief official and one of the local doctors.

Tom suddenly changed direction and walked hurriedly away with the doctor, disappearing through a side door, just as Hin guided her through another door and out into a long corridor.

Before she had time to wonder what was going on, the chief official was next to her and handing her some scissors.

'He wants you to cut the ribbon on the machine,' Hin translated as another door was opened.

Bec walked into the X-ray room and stood before the much-coveted, shiny new machine.

The staff looked eagerly at her. A nervous patient sat waiting for his chest X-ray.

She smiled, nodding at Hin to translate. 'It is my pleasure to observe the first X-ray being taken.' She snipped the ribbon.

Everyone clapped and she was ushered into the anteroom.

With much fanfare the X-ray was taken.

And another.

An hour later Bec had observed twelve X-rays being taken and talked to each of the patients. She had a sudden flash of insight into the duties of dignitaries. Her face ached from smiling, her dress stuck to her and she had blisters on her feet.

'What happens next?'

Hin smiled. 'They show you the X-rays and then we have tea.'

'But shouldn't Tom be reading the X-rays?' She hadn't seen him since he'd walked through a different door.

'He isn't here. There's been a motorbike accident.'

The windows rattled as the wind whipped the building. 'Has he gone to the emergency department? Do they need my help?'

Hin shrugged. 'He went in the ambulance.'

'In this weather?' A slither of fear raced through her. She pushed it down.

'You just have to look interested at the X-ray picture,' Hin instructed her mildly, ignoring her question.

Resigned, she turned to face the light box as three chest films were clipped into place and proudly displayed. All films showed evidence of the damage coal dust could do to lungs, fibrous lung tissue making gas exchange difficult and breathing increasingly hard.

The light box suddenly buzzed and went black.

An almighty crack boomed around the room as Bec realized that lightning must have struck the building. The room went black. An ear-splitting crash followed. Rain poured through the roof as the ceiling curled back, ripped open like a sardine can. The wind swirled in, sucking up everything in its path, the noise deafening.

She instinctively reached out, trying to find Hin. Trying to remember the layout of the room. 'I don't think this is the edge of a typhoon,' she yelled over the roar of the wind as fear clawed at her.

Tom was out in this storm.

CHAPTER ELEVEN

TOM CROUCHED UNDER a plastic sheet held up by two men to protect him and his patient from the blinding rain. It wasn't really working. He was as wet as if he'd just got out of a pool. Water dripped off his hair as he shone his torch into the eyes of a young man who had lost control of his motorbike.

The road, if it could be called that, was now almost mud. The bike had gone into a wild skid, and both rider and bike had crashed into a ditch. He'd been pulled out of the water-filled trough by passers-by and now lay by the side of the road.

Tom prayed he had no spinal damage that had been made worse by the rescue attempts of his friends. Squinting in the rain, he watched for pupil contractions in response to the light. Sluggish.

Not good. The law in Vietnam was that riders on country roads had to wear helmets. Unfortunately, this young man had been on a back road up by the mine and hadn't worn his.

Tom had come ahead in the four-wheel-drive as the ambulance hadn't been able to negotiate the back road.

Even the truck had struggled. He'd arranged to meet the ambulance at the village further down the mountain.

He needed to combine thoroughness with speed.

'What's your name?' he asked the patient, as part of checking his mental status.

'Loc.' The man grimaced as he tried to move.

'Where does it hurt, Loc?' Tom sat back on his haunches.

The young man closed his eyes. 'Head.'

Tom put his hand on Loc's shoulder. 'Try and stay awake, Loc. Where else does it hurt?'

'Everywhere.'

Tom sighed and started a comprehensive examination as water from the tarpaulin cascaded down his back. He needed to get Loc into the vehicle but couldn't move him until he'd examined him fully.

Thunder echoed around him as the wind increased in velocity, blowing the rain nearly horizontally. He glanced up at the bare hills. At least there were no trees for the wind to bring down on them. If this storm was the edge of a typhoon, he'd hate to be any closer.

Loc held his left arm close to his body, almost cradling it with his other hand.

Tom's fingers expertly palpated Loc's clavicle, finding the telltale lump of a fracture. He continued down the arm, checking for a fractured humerus, radius and ulnar. Those three bones were intact.

'You've broken your bone here.' Tom gently placed his fingers on Loc's collarbone. He slipped a triangular sling into place, pulling it up high so the weight of Loc's arm would pull the fractured bone into alignment.

'Can you feel this?' He put his hands on Loc's feet. Loc nodded.

'Good. Wiggle your toes.'

The young man tried and yelped in pain.

Tom picked up the shears from his emergency kit and cut Loc's jeans straight up on both sides, and started examining his legs. His right leg was at a distorted angle.

My father pushed me down a flight of stairs fracturing every bone in my leg.

Bec's voice crowded in on his thoughts. He forced it away as his guilt flared. He'd hurt her badly but he'd had no other choice. It was either hurt her now or hurt her even more later. He couldn't give her false hope.

He could only offer her friendship. She wanted more than that. But his energies belonged to Vietnam, and finding his mother.

All through the ceremony he'd felt her large, expressive eyes on him. He'd wanted to hide, knowing she could see more than he'd ever revealed to anyone. This callout had been a relief for both of them, breaking up an excruciating situation.

'You've broken one of the bones in your right leg. I'm going to tie your leg to a board and then we'll carry you to the vehicle.' He wished he had a Donway splint but all he had was a backboard and some crêpe bandages.

Loc started to shiver, his shoulders shuddering as shock set in.

Tom sighed as he strapped Loc's leg to the board. The poor guy would be in agony travelling over the rough roads. He couldn't give him anything for pain because he didn't want to mask any symptoms of a head injury or a slow bleed into his brain. He didn't even have any dry clothing for the poor guy. Or himself.

'OK, we need to carry Loc to the four-wheel-drive.' Tom stood up and instructed the men, demonstrating how two of them could make a chair with their hands. 'I will support his leg.'

Rumbling thunder sounded again. A niggling sense of unease rolled through him. 'On my count.'

Loc groaned as they carried him to the vehicle. Mud stuck to Tom's shoes, clawing at the soles, sucking at his feet and making walking difficult. They loaded him into back of the truck and Tom inserted an intravenous drip.

'We can go now,' he called out to the driver as he taped the drip into place, hanging the bag from the coat hanger clip. 'Take it easy, though.'

The windscreen wipers could barely keep the rain at bay. Visibility was poor. The truck skidded and slid as they edged toward the village.

It was the longest twenty minutes of Tom's life but finally they came off the mountain and into the village. They transferred Loc into the waiting ambulance. Tom walked toward the front of the vehicle and was about to swing up into the front seat when he heard a frantic voice calling, *'Bác sĩ.'*

He turned to see a woman running toward him.

'You must see my daughter. She is very sick.'

Tom leaned through the open door, back toward the ambulance officer. 'I need to see this patient. Can you wait?'

Worry lines creased the man's forehead. 'The roads are bad, we should go now.'

The woman tugged his arm. 'She needs a doctor.'

Torn, Tom flicked open his phone. He had a signal. 'You take Loc to hospital. If I need you back, I'll ring.'

'Yes, Doctor.' The driver started the ignition and slowly turned toward the main road.

Tom followed the woman toward the back of the village where the houses nestled against the base of the mountain. He struggled to walk against the gale-force winds, keeping his head down against the rain. Water covered his feet.

The deep rumbling he'd heard halfway up the mountain when he'd been treating Loc sounded louder.

Sounded longer.

Suddenly it didn't sound anything like thunder. It sounded more like the roar of crashing boulders and cracking tree trunks.

The water that covered the track changed, getting higher and thicker.

Mud.

Moving mud.

His head shot up. The rain-saturated soil was giving way. A wall of mud was rushing down the mountain toward them, bringing everything in its path along with it.

His heart pounded against his chest. *Move to higher ground.* He grabbed the woman by the arm. 'Mud-slide.'

She pulled against him. 'My daughter.'

Her hand slipped out of his wet grasp as the wave of mud rolled against him, hitting him at waist height and pushing him off balance.

He heard her scream as a tree trunk hit her, pushing her under. *No!*

Keep upright.

Trees, boulders, mud and sand swept down in a thunderous roar, swirling around him, knocking his feet out from under him.

Instructions from white-water rafting boomed in his head. *Feet first. Protect your head.*

With superhuman strength he pushed himself around so his feet were facing down the mountain. Mud sucked at him, threatening to suffocate him. *Keep your head up.*

Mud reached his chin. He could taste it on his lips.

Death by drowning in mud.

Terror consumed him as every survival instinct kicked in.

I'm here and I love you. Bec's soft, determined voice called to him. *Take a chance with me.*

Visions of his parents flashed through his mind, their love for him vivid on their faces.

You've been blessed, Tom Bracken.

He caught sight of a coconut palm.

Do not die.

One chance. He had one chance if he could get to the tree. One chance if the tree was sturdy enough to withstand the mudflow.

You've woven a dream around a family you wanted to find.

He couldn't die. He had real people who loved him.

The people who had made him the man he was. People he'd foolishly turned his back on in his quest.

He had Bec. He needed Bec. He wanted a chance with her.

He loved her.

By hell, he was going to live and tell her.

Using his arms and feet, he tried to move against the tide, praying the mud would carry him into the tree, not past it.

He lunged, wrapping his arms and legs around the trunk.

Mud cascaded over his head, seeping into his nose, his eyes, clogging his throat, forcing his body hard against the tree. The trunk moved underneath him, bowing over under his weight.

His chest burned.

His head started to spin, sparks of light flickered against the blackness of his mind.

Bec's image came into his mind with three-dimensional clarity. Wearing her bikini, her body pressed against his, her smiling face laughing up at him, and her arms wrapped tightly around his waist. He could feel her, touch her and taste her.

Slowly her image faded.

His arms slipped.

A bright whiteness beckoned in the distance.

Bec held a torch while a doctor stitched Hin's arm in the emergency department. He'd been injured by flying debris when the roof had ripped off the X-ray department.

Human injuries had been minor. Machine injury had been worse. The rain had flooded the room and the shiny new X-ray machine had taken a battering. As had the main power supply when it had been struck by lightning.

The staff at the hospital had immediately switched into emergency procedures. The hum of generators provided some power but for fine work, torches were needed.

The ambulance officer came through the door, wheeling in a young man with a broken leg.

Bec immediately looked beyond them for Tom.

No one was behind them. Anxiety skittered through her. 'Hin, can you ask where Tom is, please?'

'Sure.' He spoke to the doctor.

The doctor spoke to the ambulance officer who replied and a nurse added something.

Frustration built in Bec. She wished she could understand.

'He stayed to see another patient. We're to pick him up on our way south,' Hin explained, grimacing as another stitch went in. He gripped Bec's hand. 'Thank you for helping me.'

'My pleasure. Now you have a story to impress the girls with when they see your scar.'

He grinned. 'Good idea.'

Bec dressed Hin's wound, apprehension swirling inside her at Tom's absence. *This is madness.* Tom didn't love her and she had to learn to separate her life from his. She had no need to be worried for him.

But she couldn't shake the trepidation that clung to her.

Noise suddenly exploded around her. Doctors and nurses started to run around frantically, hauling equipment from cupboards, calling out instructions to each other.

'Hin, what's going on?' She watched the colour drain from his face.

He reached out his hand, holding hers. 'The rain has caused a mudslide at the village where Tom stayed.'

Mudslide! She breathed deeply, trying not to panic. 'So he's been in contact, requesting the ambulance? Requesting medical supplies?'

Hin shook his head slowly. 'The village has been destroyed. We don't know what is happening down there but we expect casualties.'

Casualties. She swayed as the meaning of Hin's words rocked through her, sending the blood rushing from her face. Tom dead. He could *not* be dead. She tore herself out of Hin's embrace. 'I have to go there, I have to find him, I have to—'

'The ambulance has left and Tom took the four-wheel-drive.'

'Then get me another one, now!' She didn't recognise the screaming voice as her own. 'If he's alive he'll be working to help the victims. He needs me. He needs us.'

Hin looked at her blankly, as if she were a crazy stranger.

Using every ounce of control she could muster, she spoke quietly and respectfully. 'This is Tom, Hin. Please, get me a vehicle.'

Ten minutes later the first truckload of villagers arrived. Covered in mud, their eyes told their story—fear intermingling with grief. They were alive but part of them was dead, traumatised by seeing loved ones snatched away from them by a deluge of life-stealing mud.

Urgency played through her. She made Hin question

every one of them but no one knew of the *Bác sĩ*. No one knew if he lived or died.

'I'm going on that truck to the village and I need you to come with me.' Bec hauled Hin outside into the rain, clutching her medical kit. 'I can help there and find Tom.'

An hour later Bec stood facing what had once been a village.

Desolation and destruction stared back at her.

She gagged.

Mud, trees and debris covered everything that had stood in its path in much the same way lava flowed from a volcano. A few people wandered around vaguely, shocked and confused. But mostly the village was eerily silent.

The survivors had been on the first truck.

She started to shake, her legs turning to rubber. Vietnam had claimed her son, interring him. He'd wanted to belong and now he was part of the country in a way no one could ever have imagined.

'Tom.' Her ragged voice echoed around her.

She started to walk forward, her chest heaving with great, racking sobs. She dragged her leg through the mud, welcoming the stabs of pain as the rest of her was numb with grief.

Ignoring Hin's pleading warning that the area was unsafe, she started to walk up the hill alongside the mudflow's distinct border. It looked like the photos she'd seen of areas after a natural disaster—trees cut off mid-trunk, trees stripped of all their foliage. Huts crushed flat as if they were cardboard cut-outs. No visible signs of life anywhere.

In the distance stood one lone coconut palm, its trunk marked with mud, indicating how high the flow had risen before falling away.

She continued walking.

Movement caught her eye.

She stopped and rubbed the tears from her eyes. Blinking, she took another look. Someone was sitting against the tree. Someone tall. Taller than the average Vietnamese.

She started to run, her medical kit banging into her back.

Tom. She tried to call out but hope and fear closed her throat. She dragged in another breath. 'Tom!'

The brown figure moved and stumbled to his feet, swaying unsteadily, waving his arm above his head.

Relief competed with joy, surging through her so strongly that she almost fell over. He was alive!

Hardly aware of the rain and the mud, she scrambled up to him.

He stood before her covered in mud, brown from head to toe. Unrecognisable. Except she'd know him anywhere. She threw herself at him, holding him close, needing to feel the rise and fall of his chest against her own. 'You're alive.'

His arms wrapped around her, their pressure weak. He sagged against her. 'I am.'

She lowered him down to the ground, her hands feverishly touching him, examining him for breaks, cuts and contusions. 'I thought...' She swallowed against the horror that had been with her since Hin had spoken the word 'mudslide.' 'I thought you'd died.'

'I couldn't die, I had too much to live for.' He gazed at her, his eyes filled with wonder, as if he didn't believe she was real. 'I was damned if I was going to die before I told you I loved you.'

I love you. Her heart soared. He loved her.

A kernel of doubt opened up. 'Are you sure you're not just saying that because you're in shock?'

He breathed in deeply, pain contorting his face as if he was mustering every last ounce of his energy. He slowly raised his hand to her cheek. 'Bec, I'm so sorry I hurt you. I was a fool. I'd been convinced for so long that my sense of displacement, the empty space inside me, was connected to not being able to find my birth mother and her family. Of missing out on my Vietnamese culture and language. But I had it all wrong. That sense of displacement was because I hadn't met you.'

He shuddered. 'It took the threat of suffocation by mud for me to realise that you filled that space. You were the missing half of me. The times I've spent with you have been the most wonderful times of my life. With you I've found contentment for the very first time.'

Tears pricked her eyes. 'But what about your search for your birth mother?'

His arm fell back as exhaustion claimed him. 'I'll still look but I know the chances are slim. If I don't find her I'll be OK with that. You were right. I have a loving family, one that I have badly ignored recently.'

She lay down next to him, holding him close. 'I never want to be this scared ever again.'

He tried to chuckle but started to cough. 'I got as close to death as I ever want to go. The one thing that kept me alive was you. You were with me as the mud washed over me. Your image, your voice, your fighting spirit and your love. You kept me alive, Bec. Thank you for rescuing me.'

'I'm glad I could return the favour.' She helped him sit up to ease the coughing. 'You taught me to trust again. You brought me back to life. I'd existed up until then. You showed me what I was missing.'

Worried eyes scanned her face. 'Will you spend your life with me, Bec?'

Her heart exploded with joy. 'Absolutely.' She hugged him tight. 'But first I want to get you to hospital and started on antibiotics. I think you're a prime candidate for inhalation pneumonia. Not to mention gangrene from those gashes.'

He leaned against her. 'That can wait ten more minutes. I want to sort out a couple of other things.'

'But, Tom…' The serious look in his eyes silenced her.

'I nearly died today with things left unsaid. I am not going to leave things unsaid again. I once told you I didn't want to have children because I had no medical history. It wasn't strictly true. You were right, I was scared. Scared of the unknown.'

He picked up her hand. 'But, Bec, I want us to be parents. I want us to share that experience. Together we're strong enough to deal with whatever comes our way. What do you think? Do you trust our relationship enough to have children?'

Warmth radiated through her, warming every part of her, bringing light to all the dark places. A family of her own. A family with Tom. 'I want us to have children. I couldn't think of anything more wonderful, but…' She thought of Minh.

'But what?' His voice sounded strained.

If their relationship was to have a chance she had to take a risk. 'I know you feel really strongly about overseas adoption but I believe we can offer a child something even your amazing parents couldn't. We can give a child the best of East and West. I will learn Vietnamese and you can teach me how to cook.' She bit her lip before jutting her chin forward. 'I want us to adopt Minh.'

'The cerebral palsy baby?' His voice was so soft she could barely hear it.

'Yes.'

He was silent for a few moments, his fingers tracing the length of hers, the mud on his forehead cracking along his concentration lines.

Bec held her breath.

He finally spoke. 'Minh will have more of a history than me. His parents' names will be on record. As he grows up he can have contact with them or with his other relatives if his parents are not alive.' He faced her, his eyes shining. 'I think that would be a wonderful thing to do.'

Relief flooded her and she flung her arms around him and kissed him. The taste of mud grounded her. 'Now, will you let me get you down the mountain to Hin and to the hospital?'

He nodded slowly as if the effort was almost too much.

She stood up and pulled Tom to his feet. Looping his arm around her shoulder, she supported her man and walked him down the mountain toward their new life.

EPILOGUE

TOM LEANED OVER the fence gazing out over the emerald green paddocks. The colour reminded him of Vietnam but, instead of rice, he stared at black and white cows.

A firm, work-worn hand clamped down on his shoulder. 'It's half an hour before Mum dishes up, son. She's cooked the works—roast lamb, baked veggies and rhubarb crumble for dessert.'

Tom turned toward his dad's tanned, smiling face. Kind sky-blue eyes looked at him from under a battered akubra hat. 'Mum always cooks that when we're heading back to Vietnam.'

His father nodded. 'She needs to send you off with your favourite meal. Besides, Minh adores Aussie lamb and this time next year the baby will be chomping it down, too.'

Tom laughed. 'You're probably right.' He walked up to the house with his dad, matching his stride. 'Minh's just blossomed on the farm this holiday. It's been a great two months, Dad, thanks.'

His dad nodded in agreement. 'We love it when you

all come to stay.' He cleared his throat. 'It's wonderful to see you so happy, Tom. Your mother and I worried about you for a long time. If we'd known you'd end up marrying Bec we could have saved ourselves a lot of sleepless nights. She's the perfect life partner for you.'

'I've been blessed, Dad. First with you and Mum adopting me, and now with Bec.'

His dad gave him a firm pat on the back.

The wire door on the farmhouse slammed open. A three-year-old boy with a rolling gait and a splint on his left leg hurtled out of the house. 'Grandpa!'

Tom's dad bent down, opening his arms as Minh raced into them, squealing with delight. 'The dog had puppies.'

'Did she, now? Well, you'd better show me, then.' He held Minh's hand and let the little boy lead him over to the shed.

Tom smiled as a childhood memory of him doing much the same thing spun through his mind.

'Penny for them.'

He looked up. Bec was leaning against a veranda post, wearing a thick Aran jumper to ward against the cold Gippsland winter evenings. Jeans clung to her legs, outlining their delicious curves, and she'd snagged her hair back in a ponytail. She looked fresh, vibrant and incredibly sexy. It was hard to believe she'd given birth to their gorgeous black-haired baby girl only six weeks previously.

He stepped up to her, leaning in close, pinning her gently to the post. He nuzzled her neck, trailing kisses along her jaw until he captured her mouth with his. 'Mmm, you taste of sugar and spice.'

'I licked the mixing bowl. Your mum made cinnamon biscuits.' She wrapped her arms around his waist. 'What were you thinking about?'

'Minh's enthusiasm for the new puppies reminded me of myself at much the same age. I can still feel my small hand inside Dad's bigger one.' He sighed at the memory.

'Do you want to stay longer?' Questioning violet eyes full of love, scanned his face.

'Yes and no. It's always hard to leave, but that's part of belonging to two countries, isn't it?' He rested his chin on her hair, breathing in her apple scent. 'It's time to introduce Lily to her other home.'

Bec nodded. 'Your mum's going to come to Hanoi for Christmas and stay a couple of months. She says babies grow so quickly and change so fast that she can't bear to miss an entire year.' She stroked his jaw. 'Your parents are the best grandparents any kid could hope for.'

'They are. I'm thinking next year we might take six months out and work from the Melbourne office. Spend a bit more time down here.' He laughed. 'Give the grandparents so much exposure to the kids they'll be putting us on the plane to Vietnam.'

He turned toward the house as the beep of the fax machine sounded. 'That will be Jason, briefing us. Hopefully, the staff for your kinder programme in Lai Chau province are trained and ready to go.'

'With Sung in charge, they'll be very well trained.' She grabbed his hand and pulled him along the veranda. 'Work starts again tomorrow but right now the baby is asleep, your mum is freshening up for dinner and Minh and your dad are in the shed.'

Heat pooled low in his belly. 'What did you have in mind?'

'I thought we had just enough time for some old-fashioned country cannoodling.' She pushed him down onto the swinging seat and sat in his lap, deliberately wriggling against him.

'Devil.' His hand shot under her jumper.

She gasped as fingers caressed her breasts. 'You're not playing fair.'

He grinned. 'Neither are you.'

She laughed, settling back against him, her head resting on his shoulder. 'I never thought life could offer me this much happiness, Tom.'

He knew exactly what she meant. His love for her had expanded daily over the past two years. She was his wife, his colleague, mother to his children, his friend and his lover. 'I give thanks every day that you walked into my life. No matter where I am in the world, with you by my side, I'm home.'

Her smiling mouth came up to meet his, her lips meeting his, infusing him with love and commitment. Promising a future together.

He sealed that promise with his kiss.

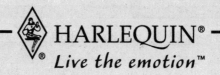

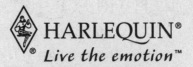

HARLEQUIN®
INTRIGUE®

BREATHTAKING ROMANTIC SUSPENSE

Shared dangers and passions lead to electrifying
romance and heart-stopping suspense!

Every month, you'll meet six new heroes
who are guaranteed to make your spine tingle
and your pulse pound. With them you'll enter
into the exciting world of Harlequin Intrigue—
where your life is on the line
and so is your heart!

THAT'S INTRIGUE—
ROMANTIC SUSPENSE
AT ITS BEST!

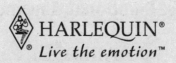

HARLEQUIN®
Live the emotion™

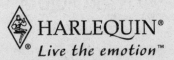